OTHERWISE **KNOWN AS**
MURDER

CHARLES SCRIBNER'S SONS

NEW YORK

MAXWELL MACMILLAN CANADA

TORONTO

MAXWELL MACMILLAN INTERNATIONAL

NEW YORK OXFORD SINGAPORE SYDNEY

●

OTHERWISE **KNOWN AS**

MURDER

A Mystery Introducing

Stokes Moran

NEIL McGAUGHEY

•

Copyright © 1994 by Neil McGaughey

Charles Scribner's Sons
Macmillan Publishing Company
866 Third Avenue
New York, NY 10022

Maxwell Macmillan Canada, Inc.
1200 Eglinton Avenue East
Suite 200
Don Mills, Ontario M3C 3N1

Macmillan Publishing Company is part of the Maxwell Communication Group of Companies.

Library of Congress Cataloging-in-Publication Data
McGaughey, Neil.
  Otherwise known as murder: a mystery introducing Stokes Moran/Neil McGaughey.
    p.   cm.
  ISBN 0-684-19674-3
  I. Title.
PS3563.C3637208   1994
813'.54—dc20   94–1527
                            CIP

Macmillan books are available at special discounts for bulk purchases for sales promotions, premiums, fund-raising, or educational use. For details, contact:

Special Sales Director
Macmillan Publishing Company
866 Third Avenue
New York, NY 10022

10   9   8   7   6   5   4   3   2   1

Printed in the United States of America

For Liz Clark,
who was the first to care;
for Sue Hathorn,
who cares too much;
and for Don,
who couldn't care less

ACKNOWLEDGMENTS

This novel is not a parody, but it is a loving tribute to all those mystery writers who have given me so much pleasure over the years.

No effort of this kind is ever possible without the invaluable contributions of other people. I would like to thank Nancy and Nolan Minton for their ceaseless prodding and constant encouragement to get the job done and Jim Colbert for his assistance and advice.

I would also like to acknowledge the support and cooperation of *The Clarion-Ledger* in Jackson, Mississippi, and in particular, book editor Orley Hood.

To Susanne Kirk, my editor at Scribners, and to Martha Kaplan, my agent, I send my grateful appreciation.

CHAPTER 1

*"Light and frothy, with a boundless energy
and infectious humor that make this novel a
treat from start to finish."*

Stokes Moran,
on *Gaylord Larsen's* A Paramount Kill

"How did you kill him?"

"With a gun."

"There's no question it's murder?"

"What do you mean?"

"It couldn't be suicide?"

"The cops don't find the gun."

"So what's your problem?"

"I can't decide if I should lock the bedroom door."

"What difference does it make?"

"It'd give me a locked-room murder."

"Can you explain it away?"

"Oh sure. I'm just not convinced it adds anything to the
mystery. I'm afraid it'll just confuse the reader."

"How far in are you?"

"About fifty pages. Is that too late for the murder?"

"You need a hook in the first ten pages."

"Look. You don't have to tell me about a hook. Who's the
expert here anyway?"

"You, of course. But you're a reviewer. This is the first time you've ever tried to write a mystery yourself. It's one thing to know how it's done, but quite another to do it."

"This was your idea in the first place. Gimme a break."

"Could I put you on hold? I've got to take an urgent call from the Coast."

I flipped to the speaker and heard that god-awful Muzak that floods the phone whenever my beautiful agent, Lee Holland, leaves me in the lurch. I hated listening to it, but at least when it shut off, I'd know Lee was back on the line. And I wouldn't have to stand there like an idiot, cradling that stupid appliance.

Let me introduce myself. I'm a nationally syndicated mystery reviewer. The byline *Stokes Moran* currently appears in more than eighty newspapers and Sunday supplements in thirty-two states. My agent says she won't be satisfied until I make every state in the union. Me, I just like the money.

And, believe me, liking money is the only reason I had agreed to this scheme in the first place. Reviewing mystery novels, at least the way I do it, is a full-time occupation, not to mention the occasional articles I submit to the mystery magazines. But my agent had guaranteed me that the first Stokes Moran mystery novel would at least bring in an advance in the high five-figures, maybe more. Which advance she was now negotiating with several editors.

But for me to free the time I needed to write the book, I had been forced to quadruple my usual output of reviews. Round-the-clock reading of unbound galley proofs can be murder on the eyes. Not to mention what it does to the back. And arms. And shoulders.

2

But last week, after a grueling and seemingly endless three months, I had finally met my goal. I had fifty reviews "in the can" for publication within the next one to six months. Which would give me at most half a year to complete work on my own murder mystery. It meant my reading public would not have to go a single week without a Stokes Moran review. And, more importantly, it meant I would not have to go a single week without a paycheck. Heaven forbid!

But the five-figure advance was not in the bank yet. And I was beginning to wonder if it ever would be.

Because I was now finding that writing a mystery was not as easy as I had thought. Over the past decade, Stokes Moran has become recognized and acknowledged as an expert in the field of mystery fiction. The name has appeared on paperback and dust jacket blurbs, in scholarly texts, and on magazine columns. It's one thing to write a five-hundred-word review but quite another a sixty- or seventy-thousand-word mystery novel. Could Stokes Moran do it? Or, the even better question, could *I* do it?

You see, Stokes Moran is only a pen name I employ for the reviews. My real name is—

"Kyle, are you there?"

I reached for the phone and lifted the receiver to my ear. "I had just about given up on you."

"That was *Playboy.* They want you to do a feature article on Seymour Severe. For their May issue. Which means you'll have to have it in by the end of the year."

I groaned. "But that's less than four weeks away. What do they expect—a miracle? Anyway, I can't spare the time, Lee. You know that."

"I know they're offering twenty-five thousand dollars. So you'll just have to find the time."

"Wow!" That figure impressed even me.

"Plus expenses."

"What expenses?"

"They want an interview."

I choked a laugh. "You've got to be kidding. How do they expect me to interview somebody who doesn't exist?"

"He exists, Kyle."

"Yeah, but nobody knows who he is, so it's almost as if he didn't exist. Seymour Severe's identity is the most closely guarded secret in the industry. I hear even his publishers don't know who he is."

"Somebody, somewhere, knows. It's just a matter of finding out."

"But why me? Why now?"

"You, because you're the best mystery critic in America. And now, because Severe's fourth novel is coming out in the spring. And they want you to review it too."

"For the same issue?"

"Yes."

"Well, that might not be possible. The publisher's not sending out any advance reading copies. I've tried for the last month to persuade them to make an exception for me, but it was a no go. They wouldn't even reveal the title. According to Severe's publicist, everything about the book is being kept under tight wraps until the book is shipped in mid-to-late April."

Lee coughed. "And that cloak-and-dagger routine, and all the publicity it'll generate, is precisely why *Playboy* wants to be the one who finally unmasks the reclusive author. It'll be a national coup."

"Do you have any idea how impossible this is going to be?"

"For twenty-five grand, I have every confidence you'll succeed."

"What about my novel?"

"It can wait."

"What!" I couldn't believe this was the same woman who had spent the last seven months first talking me into the idea of writing a mystery and then helping me work out the logistics of keeping my reviews flowing while I wrote the damn book. Or attempted to, that is. "You were all hot and bothered for it just five minutes ago."

"Well, send me what you've done. Then put it aside for a little while. Or, better yet, work on the two together. After all, how long could it take to track down one measly writer?"

Yes, I wondered, how long indeed.

CHAPTE**R** 2

*"Charming characterization, witty dialogue,
challenging puzzle. And enough mystery trivia
to satiate even the most ravenous mystery
appetite."*

—*Stokes Moran,
on Carolyn G. Hart's* Deadly Valentine

Two weeks—two frustrating, fruitless weeks—and I was no
closer to discovering Seymour Severe's identity than I had
been at the start. And all the while my mystery novel was lan-
guishing in what can only be called a Severe slump.

No one knew who this guy was. None of my publishing contacts—and they number in the dozens—had been of any help
at all. Endless conversations with agents, booksellers, even
Severe's fellow mystery writers, had yielded nothing. Tracking
down his number-one fan, a Midwestern woman who had
authored numerous critical assessments of Severe's work and
who published a quarterly Severe newsletter, added little to
what I already knew. The man was a friggin' ghost.

I did learn what he was not, however. Rumors for years had
speculated that Pulitzer-Prize winner Nolan Sender hid
behind the Severe crime de plume, but every knowledgeable
person I spoke with adamantly denied this. For one thing, by
way of dismissal, they all agreed Severe writes better.

So, all I had was a brief capsule. Seymour Severe had burst on the American mystery scene with the publication of his first Giles Manning adventure, *The Bloodless Streets*, almost fifteen years ago. But in that relatively short time span, with only two more Giles Manning mysteries to his credit, Seymour Severe had changed the course of fictional crime writing and had become the unchallenged master of the genre. And he had built that reputation while remaining totally invisible.

All that was known about him was the little I had learned the very first day of my search. Seymour Severe is a pseudonym; he has no agent; his manuscripts arrive at his publisher unannounced; his royalties are deposited into a numbered bank account in the Cayman Islands; all communication with him is done through classified advertisements in the *Atlanta Journal-Constitution*. It reads more like something out of a spy novel than a business transaction.

I unearthed one interesting tidbit of information near the end of the second week. I was talking by phone with Severe's editor's secretary (something akin to Lincoln's doctor's dog, I suppose) when she revealed that the envelopes his manuscripts arrived in were always postmarked New Orleans.

Which came as no great surprise. All three of the Giles Manning novels take place in New Orleans, and I had already surmised that Severe either lived in or near the Big Easy at one time or another in his life. But that didn't help much, considering millions of people could make the same claim.

So, after dozens of phone calls, and untold hours of library research, I was basically right back where I started.

Nowhere.

* * *

"Lee, I don't see any way this is going to happen. I'm running out of time, so I think you better call *Playboy* and get me out of this."

"Look, Kyle, you don't want me to call *Playboy*. I sent them the first part of your mystery, and they want to run an excerpt."

"Great. Then we can forget Severe."

"No such luck. They are only interested in the novel as a follow-up to the exposé. No Severe, no *Playboy*."

"Then come up with something brilliant."

"I don't have anything brilliant. But I do think you ought to follow the trail where it leads."

"You mean New Orleans?"

"Yes. You told me that's where the manuscripts are mailed from."

"But that doesn't mean Severe necessarily lives there."

"True. But do you have anything better to go on?"

"No," I admitted. "But it's a long way from Connecticut to go on such a slim possibility."

"It's either that, or give up the *Playboy* deal."

"Then I guess I'm on my way to New Orleans."

"I knew you'd see it my way." I could hear the smug self-satisfaction in her voice.

"Make the reservations for me," I said irritably. "Since *Playboy*'s paying, book everything first class. And get me a room at the Queen Royale in the French Quarter. Severe has mentioned that hotel in all three of his books. Who knows, I might get lucky."

"Consider it done. And which name do you want to use on this little excursion—Stokes Moran or Kyle Malachi?"

I weighed the alternatives. "Better use Moran. I like the irony of it. One pseudonym going after another."

Lee laughed. "Yeah, it is an intriguing scenario. But, Kyle," Lee paused, "be careful."

"What are you talking about?"

"I don't know. It just seems to me that anyone who has gone to such extremes to conceal his identity might not exactly welcome your interest. You don't know what he might be hiding."

She had a point, one that I had not considered until that moment. Why would Seymour Severe be so determined in preventing the world from knowing who he was? What was he concealing?

Dammit, who was he?

* * *

The lady sitting across the aisle from me gripped a paperback copy of Seymour Severe's *Dreamers Die Dirty*. I could see the blurb on the back cover that heralded the novel as "monumental, gripping, an extraordinary achievement in storytelling." I was tempted to reach across, tap the lady on the shoulder, and inform her those were my words, but she'd probably only have called the flight attendant for protection from a passenger gone berserk. Also, I was afraid her carry-all, teetering on her lap and filled to overflowing with Christmas packages, would topple and scatter its contents all over creation if I interrupted her reverie. So I just sat quietly and kept the information to myself. Which was probably for the best, since most people are not impressed by leeches anyway. Over the years I've modified that old saw: "Those who can, write; those who can't write, edit; and those who can't write or edit become critics."

My briefcase sat on my lap, though not as precariously as the lady's satchel in hers. In it was page after page of what I was optimistically calling my mystery novel. Who was I kidding? I'm no writer. I couldn't sustain more than a thousand words if my life depended on it. All I know how to do is compose short, pithy sentences that look good on the covers of cheap paperbacks. I'm little more than a hack. Who am I to think I belong in the same league as Raymond Chandler, Dashiell Hammett, James Crumley, or Seymour Severe? If they saw the pile of crap in my briefcase, they'd laugh me off the planet.

I don't normally indulge in such self-denigration. But here it was just four days away from Christmas, and I was heading in the opposite direction from where I wanted to be and doing the exact thing I didn't want to do.

What I really wanted was to be at home in Connecticut, in front of a fire, writing pad placed comfortably on my knee, and dog situated familiarly at my feet. Especially the latter. I realized it was Bootsie, Irish setter extraordinaire, that was the real source of my funk.

I was feeling guilty. Guilty. GUILTY. Bootsie hates it when I board her at the kennel. Spoiled by free run of both home and yard, she can get downright psychotic when sentenced to a cage. The only thing lightening my present mood was anticipating her eager and forgiving welcome on my return. I sent her a silent promise that I'd hurry.

I pictured her as I'd seen her this morning, running in the

park beside the river, her red coat shining in the winter sun, tail flapping excitedly against the wind, barking wildly at the ducks along the water's edge.

"Sir?"

I startled awake. The flight attendant leaned over me.

"Yes?"

"You missed the notice to fasten your seat belt. We'll be landing in New Orleans in just a few minutes."

* * *

I've never been to New Orleans when it didn't rain, and this time was no different. As I stepped from the protection of the terminal building, I was met by a whipping December spray more appropriate to the coasts of Alaska than to the tropical climes of southern Louisiana. So much for the effusively generous guidebooks that promised a winter respite from the frigid conditions of the Northeast. Send me back to Connecticut. Luckily, I had watched the Weather Channel while I was packing and was wearing my heaviest winter topcoat. But I still shivered in the cold.

"Ain't no more cabs," the skycap called from the relative protection of his tiny cubicle. He looked wedged in. How he had managed to squeeze his large frame into the small space seemed to defy the rules of volume and mass. "Lotta dee-laze tonight. More'n a dozen cabs usually. But two planes come in 'bout the same time. And now all gone. All gone." Gesturing at the empty cab stands and grinning more to himself than to me, the man kept mumbling "All gone. All gone." I wondered if all skycaps weren't a little bit crazy at 2 A.M. Or was it just New Orleans that did this to you?

"How can I get downtown?" I yelled into the wind.

"Phone's inside." He nodded toward the concourse. "But it'll probably take an hour for 'em to send a cab out. The reg'lars should be back by then."

Drenched and chilled to the bone, I carted my two bags and briefcase (why had I brought so much?) back inside the airport and looked for a pay phone. Spotting one on the opposite side of the concourse, I made my slow and cumbersome way over to it only to discover the directory had been ripped from its cover. All that was left was the empty hardcover shell.

"This is not my day," I muttered under my breath. I dialed operator assistance, got the number for a local company, and was told it would be at least forty-five minutes before they could get a taxi out to me. I told them to forget it and went in search of a car-rental counter.

* * *

The Queen Royale is situated in the heart of what the locals simply call the Quarter. The hotel's elegant charm and studied dignity belie its location in the midst of what's probably the most decadent and depraved square mile south of Times Square. You'd expect any other hotel and any other city to be quietly slumbering at three-fifteen in the morning. But not the Queen Royale. And certainly not the Quarter.

I had experienced no difficulty in following the rental clerk's directions in locating the hotel. The Buick Regal they had assigned me had added no additional complications to my journey. So I stepped off the elevator from the parking garage feeling more optimistic than I'd felt since leaving home.

As I entered the lobby, I viewed a vast expanse of red, green, gold, and white. Glittering streamers hung from the ceiling; hundreds of poinsettias covered every available flat surface. Four massive Greek columns were circled with tinsel and baby's breath. I noticed a man lounging against one of the columns. He was dressed all in white, somewhat odd for December, even in New Orleans, and he stood out in stark contrast to the Christmas colors. I could feel his eyes on me as I crossed to the reservations desk. A miniature Christmas tree greeted me, and bunting behind the clerk wished me Happy Holidays. Some female singer was mutedly "Walking in a Winter Wonderland" and was just about to be married by Parson Brown. As I waited for my reservation to be verified, I turned to look at the man in white.

I judged him to be about my age, maybe a little older, maybe pushing forty with somewhat more vigor than I. And maybe battling it with a fiercer determination as well. Lee's warning had made me too suspicious. Surely this man was just scouting the new arrivals *(at this hour?)* and had no particular interest in me *(then why had his eyes never left me?)*. But he continued to stare, until our eyes finally locked. There was no smile, no gesture of greeting. Unlike most people, he did not hurriedly shift his gaze away when caught in the act. I too refused to back down and kept my eyes riveted to his. Ridiculously, this had turned into a contest of wills. Who would be the first to look away? I felt grotesquely exposed for some reason, but I used the opportunity to study the man anyway.

He looked a lot like me. I wondered if his eyes saw, as mine did, a man who still had the good looks of youth, still trim and fit after almost four decades of life? Or did he just see a six-foot frame topped by a mane of unruly sandy hair? Or was he appraising the off-the-rack clothes and estimating the cost? Or was he looking beyond the clothing?

"You're in Suite Four Twenty-One, Mr. Moran." The desk clerk's voice pulled me around, forcing me to concede the childish game to the man in white. "Sign here, please."

I dutifully signed the register. "I'm sure I didn't reserve a suite." Even with *Playboy* picking up the tab, Lee never would have been so extravagant. Agent penury runs deep, no matter who's paying.

"All our rooms are called suites, sir," the clerk responded. I glimpsed his Christmas suspenders as he leaned forward to tap the bell.

"Donny," he called. I half-expected to see the man in white answer the summons, but surely bellhops don't dress so elegantly? But it was a much younger man, looking like little more than a teenager in his regulation uniform, who abruptly materialized at my elbow. "Take Mr. Moran's things up to Four Twenty-One." I noticed the clerk had dropped the suite part.

"Yessir." I followed the bellboy to the elevators and then to my room. And to blissful sleep.

CHAPTER 3

*"Dark and brooding like the twilight along
the Mississippi River."*

—*Stokes Moran,*
on *Julie Smith's* New Orleans Mourning

I slept until ten, then ordered room service. Since I had
absolutely no idea how to proceed, I really didn't want to face
the day.

Why was I doing this anyway, I asked myself for perhaps the
hundredth time since I'd foolishly agreed to this harebrained
scheme. I didn't particularly relish the idea of invading another man's privacy. Seymour Severe had gone to a lot of trouble
to conceal his identity. If by some chance I did manage to track
him down, what gave me the right to expose him?

I certainly hoped it was not for the money. I live comfortably enough on what I make as a mystery reviewer; I didn't
actually need the extra dough, but then, nobody turns down
twenty-five grand. Not if they have a lick of sense in their
heads, that is. And, while the *Playboy* exposure would be nice,
I am already nationally known; of course, I'd hate to lose the
magazine notoriety, but I could live without it.

So, I concluded, my reason had to be the challenge, the
matching of wits. With Severe going to such elaborate pains to
hide himself, the man was just asking for somebody to come

along and uncover him. I decided that "somebody" might just as well be me.

And I couldn't discount the mystery of it either. Ever since I was a kid, I'd hated unanswered questions and unsolved riddles. Maybe that was why I loved mystery fiction so much. From Conan Doyle to Sue Grafton, you could always count on a final resolution.

I rehashed all these thoughts as I shaved and showered. I was just pulling on my bathrobe when I heard a knock at the door. It was the bellboy from last night, carrying my breakfast tray. He strode into the room and placed the tray down on the table next to my bed. I signed the check he put in front of me and added a sizable tip. Why not let *Playboy* win friends and influence people for me?

"It's Donny, right?" I asked as I returned the bill to him.

"Yessir." He stood facing me like a soldier at attention, his muscles rigid. His close-cropped blond hair reinforced the military image.

"Are you always on duty?"

"I'm working a double shift this week, sir."

I admired his stamina. "Ah yes, the energy of youth. I remember it well." I smiled, encouraging a like response from him. But he just stood there, staring myopically ahead. For some reason, I felt unnerved. "Look," I said, "maybe you can help me. I'm trying to find someone, a writer named Seymour Severe." What could it hurt to be up front about this? It wasn't like I was on some secret mission. "Ever heard of him?"

"No sir."

"I have a hunch he lives here in the French Quarter. Do you have any suggestions on where I should start looking?"

For the first time, his features became energized, as if waiting for this cue. "Well, sir," this wannabe soldier came to parade rest, "Fido's is a favorite hangout."

"Fido's? What's Fido's?"

"It's a bar off Bourbon. 'Bout three blocks from here. Doesn't open till midnight though."

I grimaced. "Any other ideas? Maybe someplace I could try during the day."

"You say he's a writer?"

"Yes. A mystery writer."

He smiled, an engagingly toothy smile that lent an attractive and vulnerable quality to his boyish face.

"Well, there's a mystery bookstore several blocks down Decatur."

"The name?"

"Murder on the Levee, I think. Or Death on the Levee. Something like that. And there are five or six other bookstores in the Quarter." He paused. "Regular ones, I mean."

I was puzzled. "Regular ones?"

Donny seemed embarrassed. "You know, sir, not the, ah, adult ones."

"Oh, I understand." In his awkwardly diplomatic way, Donny was cautioning me about the pornographic wares that proliferate the French Quarter, especially Bourbon Street.

"Anything else, sir?"

"No." I followed Donny to the door.

"Enjoy your breakfast, sir."

"Thank you, Donny." I reached for the door to shut it behind him.

He turned to leave, then swiveled back, and anxiously

whispered, "This writer, sir. If you don't mind my asking, what do you want him for?"

I didn't think any damage would be done by sharing the purpose of my visit with this intense young man. "I'm working for a national magazine. They want me to do an interview."

"Nothing else?" he asked.

"No, that's it."

He gravely nodded his head. "I see, sir." This time he did leave, and I closed the door.

Strange kid, I thought. So regimented, so controlled. It was indeed as if he were in the Army. But he had given me a couple of leads; whether they would be of any help was yet to be seen. Fido's and bookstores. And one a mystery bookstore. That sounded like a fun place to start. I'd check it out as soon as I dressed.

* * *

I stopped at the front desk to get directions to the mystery bookstore from this morning's clerk, an attractive brunette in her mid-thirties who confirmed that the store was indeed called Murder on the Levee. After committing her instructions to memory, I stepped out into the dank noon of the New Orleans day. It wasn't raining, so I supposed I should be grateful for small favors. It was still cold, however, and I was again thankful I had thought to bring my topcoat. I snuggled deeply into it to shield me as much as possible from the chilly wind that carried a piercing icy mist on its crest.

The number of hardy individuals braving the disagreeable elements surprised me. Maybe it was Christmas shoppers or maybe it was just normal, no matter what the temperature, for crowds to populate the French Quarter. But whatever the reason, I had to thread my way carefully through throngs of people.

The sights, sounds, and smells of the Quarter greeted me, entranced me. Many shops were dressed for Christmas, with blinking lights and holiday colors. Norfolk pines decorated for the season dotted the sidewalks. Santa's helpers rang bells soliciting donations for the needy. "Silent Night" competed with "When the Saints Go Marching In," both set to a decidedly New Orleans jazz beat. The smells of cotton candy, evergreen, coffee, and Creole cooking spiced the air.

After walking several blocks toward the river, I turned left on Decatur, which put me parallel to the river. I denied myself the pleasure of stopping at the French Market with its wonderful aroma and exotic items, noting in passing the colorful and vocal nature of the milling shoppers.

Ever get that eerily uncomfortable feeling that you're being followed? When the flesh along your spine tightens and your neck hairs do handstands? Well, I experienced those exact sensations at that moment. Twice as I trudged down Decatur, I turned to see if I could spot anyone trailing me. A useless effort, really, more automatic than anything else, since I'd have no means of recognizing any of these people, anyway. Unless they were as obvious about it as had been the man in white last night.

The man in white. That was the first time I had thought about him since our encounter. I wondered if he could be following me.

But each time I looked behind me, I could not tell that anyone seemed particularly suspicious or all that interested in me or my movements. There were no sudden about-faces or quick dartings into doorways. I put the feeling down to nerves, to reading too many mystery novels, and to Lee's rampant paranoia. Which I had to admit was contagious. But I could not shake the certainty that there was somebody back there, silently shadowing me.

Not far from where the French Market ended, I spotted Murder on the Levee on the opposite corner. Behind it, hiding the mighty Mississippi from view, was a twenty-foot seawall.

I crossed the intersection, and the instant I entered the small shop I felt back in familiar territory. Shelf after shelf held hardcover mysteries, some new, some long out of print. Since many were in protective wrappers, I spotted what I knew would be rare and expensive first edition copies of Agatha Christie, Erle Stanley Gardner, Dorothy L. Sayers, Raymond Chandler, and many other personal favorites. I could easily spend the rest of the day here, happily engrossed in this enchanting world. But I had a purpose to accomplish first.

Santa Claus sat behind the counter. Or his double, that is. A middle-aged man, with the girth and white beard to challenge St. Nick, held a copy of James Lee Burke's *Black Cherry Blues*. He stood at my approach.

"All you need," I kidded, "is the red suit."

"I save that for Christmas Eve," he joked back. "I've even got the Ho-Ho-Ho down pat." His whole body shook with the guttural effort. "Now what can I do for you?"

I decided point-blank would be best. "Do you know Seymour Severe?"

"But of course," he said.

CHAPTER 4

*"Following in the illustrious footsteps of
Raymond Chandler and Ross Macdonald,
the author has crafted an intricate thriller,
with layer upon layer of deceit and corrup-
tion."*

—Stokes Moran,
on Robert J. Ray's Merry Christmas,
Murdock

My elation at thinking I'd located the elusive Severe disappeared with the man's next words.

"Just like I know all the greats—Edgar Allan Poe, Dashiell
Hammett, Cornell Woolrich, S. S. Van Dine, Ellery Queen."

The man seemed genuine enough, and there was a very lik-
able and friendly quality about him. But I couldn't escape the
feeling that I was being toyed with, that his response had been
purposely planned first to raise my hopes and then to dash
them. Maybe it was the teasing smile that he couldn't quite
banish from the corners of his lips that convinced me I was
being had. On the other hand, maybe it was just his Santa per-
sona.

But if it was a game, I decided to join the fun.

"I'm Stokes Moran," I said, and before I could form another word, the man nearly vaulted over the counter, quite an

agile feat for a man his size, grabbed my right hand and arm, and began pumping furiously.

"This is indeed an honor, sir," he said. "I'm a big fan of yours, I've read your reviews for years. I can't tell you how pleased I am to have you in my humble establishment."

I thought that "humble establishment" routine a bit much, and it was easy to ascribe it to what was perhaps his natural-ly jovial disposition. But I still couldn't shake the feeling that this whole scene was being staged. But why? And for what purpose? And, perhaps most importantly, by whom?

"Well, thank you, Mr.—" I paused for him to fill in the blank, which he did.

"Manny Gillis, Mr. Moran. Owner and operator of Murder on the Levee. What do you think of my little place here?"

This hayseed act was getting tiresome, but I couldn't be sure if it was specifically scripted for me, or if all tourists got the same treatment.

"Well, Mr. Gillis—"

"Manny, please."

"Well, Manny, I love your store," I answered, quickly glanc-ing around. "And I would certainly love to spend the rest of the day here." He smiled at the compliment. "But," I continued, "that's not why I'm here. I'm trying to track down Seymour Severe. I'm pretty sure he lives here in New Orleans, and I thought you might be able to help me locate him."

He didn't respond immediately, so I added lamely, "Since you own a mystery bookstore."

Manny Gillis walked back behind his counter and looked at me appraisingly. It gave me the opportunity to return the favor.

I realized that my earlier assessment of him as middle-aged had been somewhat off the mark. Up close his face showed the lines of age and his hands bore the telltale signs of liver spots. But his eyes held an intensity that spoke of repressed energy, perhaps even hostility. I concluded that Manny Gillis was a man neither easily characterized nor categorized. Maybe a dangerous man as well, despite the benign appearance. Be careful, I inwardly warned.

"You may be right about Severe living here in New Orleans." He finally spoke, leaning casually against the rear counter, arms crossed over his chest. "Though I doubt he lives in the Quarter. We're a small, closed community, and I know just about everybody down here." He paused. "Yes, I'd be very surprised if Severe lives in the Quarter." He chuckled and his belly heaved. The Santa Claus image was stronger than ever. "I'd say somebody like Severe would more probably choose the Garden District. That would fit in with his prosperity. And his stature. Though I don't know for sure. I've never met him, but I agree that his books show a familiarity with this city that only a resident would have."

His speech finished, he waited for me to respond. But before I could say anything, the door through which I'd entered crashed open, and a woman stormed in. Outrageously dressed, coiffed, and made up, she looked like something out of an all-night Halloween movie marathon, or off an Andy Warhol poster.

"Manny," she screeched. "You tell Matty to stay away from Donny. He's my son, and I don't want him mixed up in Matty's—" She spotted me and stopped in mid-sentence.

Gillis seemed totally nonplussed by her arrival. Clearly agitated, he turned to me. "Mr. Moran, this is Minerva, our local, ah, character. Minerva, this is Stokes Moran, the book critic." The way he stressed book critic sounded almost like a signal. But Minerva wasn't picking up on it, if that's what it was.

"Stow the amenities, Manny. You just remember what I said. Keep Matty away from Donny, or I will." With that, she turned and departed as abruptly as she'd come.

"What was all that?" I asked, after the door banged shut behind her.

"Nothing," Manny said. "That's just Minerva's way. Likes to make a theatrical production out of everything. She's a little bit crazy, especially when she's high. Don't pay any attention to her." I noticed a slight twitch under his left eye. His actor's mask had slipped just marginally, just enough for a facial muscle to betray his anxiety. Something told me I had just witnessed a scene that hadn't been scripted, that had not been meant for my eyes. I wondered how significant its meaning could be.

"Who's Matty?"

"Another local character. The French Quarter is loaded with them." He lifted his index finger near his right temple and performed a triple circle in the air, indicating loony land. "Look, forget Minerva. If she latches on to you, she can be a royal pain." He picked up some books from the counter and turned to shelve them. He obviously wanted the conversation dropped.

"She seemed really worried about her son," I said.

My persistence broke his composure. "Look, you don't know anything about her. Donny's not her son, for one thing." Under his breath he muttered, "In her dreams, maybe." Then louder, he concluded, "Things aren't always what they seem."

"What do you mean?"

"Do I have to paint you a picture?" he said, irritation clearly present in his voice. "You weren't born yesterday. You saw her. Minerva couldn't have a son if she wanted to. She doesn't have the right equipment."

* * *

I left the bookstore a few minutes later, never having had a chance to really investigate the stock. As an avid mystery fan, I am also a rabid collector. And normally I would not miss an opportunity to add to my collection. But today was not the time. I had other things on my mind.

The rain had returned in full gale. With no umbrella, I turned up my coat collar, hunkered my head against the sleeting wind, and sprinted from block to block, seeking momentary relief from the rain under the occasional building overhang.

But I barely noticed the miserable conditions, since I was still puzzled by the whole farce that had played itself out at Murder on the Levee. It had clearly been orchestrated, even rehearsed. I felt that everything up until Minerva's entrance had been staged for my benefit. But why, and by whom? I had asked myself these questions before but still had no satisfactory answers. The one possibility that occurred to me was that Seymour Severe was behind it. Could Manny Gillis possibly be the reclusive author? It didn't seem likely. I had never pictured Severe as remotely resembling Gillis. On the other hand, Severe's fictional detective was named Giles Manning. Manny Gillis—Giles Manning. The names seemed too similar to be mere coincidence. But then, how was I to know? Writers hide behind all sorts of masks.

And why the elaborate put-on? If that's what it was? Could Gillis have known I was coming? Was he trying to throw me off the scent because I'd gotten too close? That didn't make sense, because as far as I knew I was absolutely nowhere.

And if Gillis wasn't Severe, then who was? Was it somebody Gillis knew, somebody he wanted to protect? Again, why?

The questions repeated over and over in my mind and dogged me all the way back to the hotel. Soaked and shivering, I finally glimpsed the approaching shelter of the Queen Royale, eagerly anticipating a hot shower and some dry clothes. The man in white stood in front of the entrance. He followed me inside.

I checked at the front desk for messages. Finding none, I turned toward the elevators. The man in white cut me off.

"Mr. Moran." Not a question, but a statement.

"Yes."

"I'd like to talk to you for a minute, if it's convenient. Could we go into the bar?"

He nodded toward the hotel's piano bar, located just off the lobby, and at this hour totally devoid of clientele. But I continued walking, not taking the direction he indicated.

"As you can see, I'm wringing wet. I've got to get out of these clothes." I reached the elevators and punched the Up button.

"I assure you this will only take a minute. Plus I think you'll be interested in what I have to say."

With a confidence born of natural leadership, he led the way into the darkened bar. As we settled into a booth at the back of the room, he said, "Oh, by the way, I'm Matthew Hedges. But you can just call me Matty. Everybody does."

28

CHAPTER 5

*"Seen through the eyes of a talented writer
and shown through the character of an
appealing detective, the American dream has
never seemed quite so alluring or quite so
false."*

—*Stokes Moran,*
on *Walter Mosley's* Devil in a Blue Dress

"Cigarette?"

He proffered a pack of Camels, the ones without the filters.
I shook my head.

"No thanks," I said. "I'm trying to quit."

Watching him light up, I felt the familiar, the overwhelming,
desire come flooding back. It was now one hundred and
eighty-six days and counting since I had put my last cigarette
down, stamped it out with a determination to finally be rid of
the habit. Rarely since then had I experienced the need to pick
one up. But at that moment, sitting in those freezing clothes,
teeth knocking and body trembling, the compulsion had never
been greater.

"You are cold," Matty observed. "Would you prefer that we
go up to your room?"

"No," I said, my jaw doing a jitterbug, "this is fine." I had
no intention of inviting this stranger into my hotel room.

"Then how about a cup of coffee?"

I nodded agreement. He got up, walked over to a coffee urn that stood at the end of the bar, took a mug, and filled it. The steam trailed after him as he headed back to the booth. I clutched the cup gratefully and breathed in the warmth.

"I'll try to get this over with quickly," he said as he resumed his seat. He leaned back against the cushioned bench and stretched his right arm along the top edge. The smoke from his cigarette wafted seductively toward me. I shuddered. For years, coffee and cigarettes had defined my existence. Having one without the other seemed incomplete.

"God, I can't stand it," I blurted. "Gimme a cigarette."

"Sure." He extended the pack, and I hungrily shook one out and leaned toward the torched lighter he held. I inhaled deeply, and the rush reached all the way to my instep.

He smiled. A warm conspiratorial smile, it animated his face. It said we were compatriots. Sure, I thought, we shared an addiction. I hoped our male bonding ended there.

The smile faded. "Look, I know why you're here. I can deliver Severe to you." He stopped.

"For ten thousand dollars," he added.

I nearly choked. "Ten thousand dollars! Are you out of your mind?"

"You're getting twenty-five. Seems only fair."

"How do you know what I'm getting?"

"I know everything."

I laughed. "I'm beginning to believe it. Just who the hell are you anyway?"

"I'm whatever people believe me to be. Some people think I'm a god, so I am. Others think I'm a devil, so I'm that too. I fill whatever role your imagination can write." He leaned back against the plastic cushion. "So how do you see me? As villain? Hero? Sinner? Or saint?"

His speech could have been lifted directly from the pages of a hard-boiled thriller—a Seymour Severe thriller, perhaps? He intrigued me. I believed he could lead me to Severe, if indeed he himself were not the mysterious author.

"I've just met you, so how can I have an opinion about you yet?"

"Oh, but you do," he retorted. "If you're honest, you've already assigned me a certain part to play. So tell me, do I get to be the good guy, or am I the body in the first chapter?"

"I don't have the faintest idea what you're talking about."

He shrugged. But his last statement couldn't have been accidental. This stranger somehow knew impossible things. Granted, a lot of people knew I was looking for Seymour Severe. I had made no secret of that. But Matthew Hedges knew how much *Playboy* had offered me for the exposé, and judging from what he'd just said, he also knew I was working on my own mystery novel. Only a handful of people were privy to those two facts, none of whom I considered in Matthew Hedges's orbit, and yet he knew. *He knew!* How?

I tried another tack. "Where do you get your information?"

"What information?" He signaled the bartender. She approached, and he ordered a double Scotch. Hedges gazed at me. "More coffee?"

I shook my head. "I'm confused and a little concerned over how much you seem to know about me."

He smiled. "Don't be. It's my business to know everything that goes on in the Quarter."

"Why's that?"

He picked up the glass the waitress had just placed in front of him and drained it. "Because I'm the king of New Orleans." He set the empty glass back on the table and abruptly stood up.

"I'll be in touch," he said, and Matthew Hedges, the man in white, walked out of the bar.

* * *

Stepping out of the shower, I toweled dry. I slipped into my terry-cloth robe. It was great to feel warm again.

I walked toward the bed. The temptation to crawl between the covers was too great to resist. I shivered beneath the cool sheets but my body heat soon changed the chill to drowsy warmth.

It was still early, not quite five o'clock. Fido's wouldn't open yet for several more hours. I could afford a nap.

But sleep evaded me. My mind darted back and forth over the incidents of the day. If this had been a mystery novel, I'd have already figured it out. But this was not fiction, and I was finding out that I was no detective. I felt lost, unprepared, in over my head. I also had the uneasy suspicion I was being manipulated, that somebody—maybe Matthew Hedges—was pulling the strings.

In my mind, I replayed my recent encounter with the enigmatic and perplexing man in white. Who was he? How was he connected to Severe? What was he up to? I felt my mind drifting.

I awoke to a window-rattling roll of thunder. I hadn't even been aware I'd fallen asleep. I reached for the clock radio and pulled it into my line of vision. It was past mid-night.

"Damn," I muttered. I jumped from the bed, all sleep banished from my body, and hurriedly dressed.

* * *

"Yes," I answered when the desk clerk asked if he could be of any assistance. "Can you tell me how to get to Fido's?"

"Fido's?" He looked puzzled. "What is Fido's?"

"I think it's a bar," I answered. "It's supposed to be someplace here in the French Quarter."

"I'm sorry, but I'm not familiar with it. Are you sure you got the name right?"

"Pretty sure." I caught sight of the bellboy Donny coming through the electronic door. "Never mind. I see someone who can help me."

I approached Donny, who was unloading luggage from a baggage cart. "Donny, can you tell me how to get to Fido's? The desk clerk didn't seem to know."

"Not many people know about the place. It keeps pretty much to itself. But the guy you're looking for would probably hang out there." He then proceeded to give me detailed and somewhat confusing directions.

"Oh, by the way, I met your mother," I said, casually assuming that this boy was the same "Donny" Minerva had mentioned.

"My mother?" A perplexed look crossed his face.

"Yes. Minerva."

The boy frowned. "Minerva's not my mother, sir. I hope she didn't cause you any problem."

I shook my head. It seemed obvious Minerva was a subject

Donny preferred to avoid. Trusting I could remember the
directions he'd given me, I uttered a quick thank you and left
the hotel to walk the few blocks to Bourbon Street. Once
again, in the rain.

* * *

The streets were crowded, even at this late hour, and, as I
turned the corner onto Bourbon Street, I could hear music and
laughter coming from the bars and bistros. I walked down the
sidewalk, weaving between clumps of people, keeping an eye
out for landmarks Donny had mentioned. One of the estab-
lishments had its doors open, and I could see a naked woman
spread-eagled on a revolving table. I hastily moved on. Finally
I spotted the Tail of the Cock restaurant, so I knew I was close.
But I couldn't remember what came after that. Was I to turn
right or left? There was supposed to be an alley nearby, but I
didn't see one.

I looked in a storefront window next door to the restaurant
while I tried to think what to do next. The display featured
drug and sexual paraphernalia, much of it in a Christmas
motif. There was a Santa Claus dummy with a giant
appendage erupting from his groin, a green-and-white paint-
ed dildo with gold tinsel hanging from its base, and a miniature Christmas tree with cock rings and condoms as
ornaments. Only in America, I thought, and then amended
that to only in New Orleans.

I had half-decided to enter the still-open shop and ask the
clerk about Fido's when, through the window's reflection, I
saw Matthew Hedges standing in a doorway, grinning at me.
I turned and approached him. "Why is it you always manage

to stay high and dry when everybody else gets soaked?" It was true. He carried no umbrella, yet his white outfit showed no indication of the rain that had saturated my clothes.

He laughed. "Just lucky, I guess. What are you doing out in this neighborhood this time of night?"

"I thought this was the shank of the evening for Bourbon Street."

"Oh it is. I just didn't picture you as a typical horny tourist."

"I'm not. I'm here looking for a bar called Fido's. But I seem to have lost my way."

The smile left his face. "Fido's, huh? Now why would you want to go to Fido's?"

I wasn't about to tell him I hoped to find Seymour Severe there, since he had a mercenary interest in seeing that I located the author only through him.

"I heard it's a very special place."

"Oh it is that." The smile returned to his face. "It very definitely is that."

"Well, will you tell me how to get there?" I was getting irritated with his smugness.

"I'll go you one better. I'll take you there." He moved out of the protection of the doorway, and I followed. The rain had stopped. Matthew Hedges had once again managed to stay dry.

He turned off Bourbon, with me following, not knowing what was in store, but determined to find out. He walked about a block and a half, stopping in front of an iron grille that protected a two-foot space between two buildings. Donny hadn't mentioned anything like this. Hedges lifted up on one side of the grille, and it opened in. A gate! It certainly hadn't looked like a gate. It had looked permanently affixed to the cement.

Hedges closed it after us, and led the way down a darkened passageway, even too narrow to be called an alley. It opened up into a cobblestoned courtyard that was completely encircled by a balustraded three-story building. It looked like a private residence, not a public bar.

"Where are we?" I whispered. It was eerily quiet. Boisterous Bourbon Street seemed a long way off.

"Fido's." With what can only be called a flourish, Hedges opened a glass-fronted door and we went in.

* * *

The interior was so dark that if not for the white suit of my guide, which miraculously absorbed illumination from somewhere, I would have been completely blind. But I stuck tight to the moving form in front of me until I heard another door open. We stood on the threshold of another room, this one not much brighter than the last, but with sufficient lighting to make out shapes. Of objects. Of people.

It was a bar, or at least it resembled one. Three round tables were situated in the middle of the floor, and a few human shapes occupied the chairs surrounding them. The bar itself took up the entire length of the far wall, and I could make out a couple of people sitting on stools. The bartender was totally lost in shadows.

If this is Fido's, I thought, what's the attraction? There was no conversation, and you could barely see your hand in front of your face. But Hedges turned to his left, away from the tables and away from the bar. He approached a man standing in one corner of the room, nodded to him, and opened the door next to which he stood. I followed closely.

We had entered a stairwell, well lit but extremely narrow. After the gloom of the preceding two rooms, I was momentarily stunned. My eyes felt like they'd received a stinging blow, and were now screaming at the sudden brightness.

"If you hadn't been with me"—Hedges turned to face me as he spoke—"that man out there would not have let you pass."

I nodded. After catching a glimpse of the man's linebacker dimensions, I had no reason to doubt Hedges's assertion.

The steep stairs ended in another doorway. Hedges opened this, and we entered yet another room, this one with a pool table, video games, and pinball machines. But no people.

"Kind of slow tonight," Hedges said. We walked the length of the room to open yet another door revealing yet another flight of stairs.

"What is this?" I demanded. "A wild goose chase?"

"We're almost there. Can't make it too easy for the rubes, now can we?" Hedges chuckled. He topped the last stair and stopped. I edged around him slightly and got my first view of Fido's.

We stood at the highest point of the room. Steps leading down from the doorway led into a horseshoe-shaped arena with several sofas placed strategically on the floor. Around the perimeter of the horseshoe was a ramp or runway, slightly lower than where we now stood but roughly eye-level to anyone positioned on the sofas. A handful of men were already seated.

I followed Hedges down the steps. He stopped at the only remaining empty sofa and motioned for me to sit next to him. I panned over the crowd but received no return glances. No one here looked especially literary. If Seymour Severe were among this group, he'd done a good job of looking nondescript.

"What would you like to drink?" Hedges asked me, drawing my attention back to him.

"I don't drink," I said.

"House rules, you've got to have something. Maybe a club soda?"

"Fine." He signaled something I couldn't understand to somebody I couldn't see, but in less than two minutes I was handed a glass of bubbly beverage. It tasted more like ginger ale than club soda, but it really didn't make that big a difference to me. Hedges sipped on what I assumed was another double Scotch. How can he drink that awful mess? I wondered.

"What happens now?" I asked. Very little conversation was coming from the other sofas. Most of the men seemed content to sit and stare into space.

"The floor show should start any minute."

Almost as if on his command stereophonic sound assaulted my ears. After a few seconds, the noise receded to acceptable limits.

I leaned over to Hedges. "They really know how to get your attention." He smiled but said nothing. I noticed that the lighting had changed, or was changing. The transition was so gradual it was almost imperceptible. But there was no question that where we sat—the orchestra pit is how I perceived it—had darkened, but the stage had grown brighter.

There was a shadowy movement just beyond the left

entrance to the stage. Within seconds a woman—garishly
made up—emerged holding a leash in her right hand. She was
wearing a halter of silver lamé and cut-off jeans. I noticed her
attire for only the briefest instant because my vision was suddenly riveted to the other end of the leash.

Emerging on stage was a man. Down on all fours, completely naked except for the collar around his neck to which
the leash was attached, he was being pulled roughly forward.
The woman held a riding crop in her left hand. With one hand
tugging at the leash, the other came down viciously across the
man's naked buttocks. He lurched forward under the blow.
She repeated this action until she had the man positioned in
the center of the runway.

Most men find it awkward, embarrassing, to look at another man naked. But curiosity usually wins out over modesty.
Just think of the surreptitious glances in the YMCA showers. I
tried not to look at the subjugated man, but the outrageous-
ness of the scene compelled my attention. I judged him to be
over thirty, but how much over was unclear. While his face was
covered with a dark beard that showed no hint of gray, his
torso was hairless.

Suddenly, another woman appeared on the opposite side of
the stage, and her "dog"—I now had a good idea why this
place was called Fido's—was definitely "in heat." He
appeared to be a little older than the first, a little beefier.

I closed my eyes. I felt light-headed, hot. I heard a buzzing
in my ears. My mouth was dry. I could barely swallow.

I turned to Matthew Hedges, tried to form words, but no
sound emerged. Shapes and sounds in the room receded, and
I plunged forward, submerging into darkness.

* * *

The night air somewhat revived me, though I was still very groggy. Somehow I found myself walking, but not completely on my own power, however. Strong arms held me up and propelled me forward. I turned my neck painfully, slowly, to my right and saw a blurred white form. Matthew Hedges? My head felt leaden, heavy. I repeated the process to my other side, but I could not control my eyes sufficiently to focus on my left-hand benefactor. I strained to clear my vision, but the effort only brought a searing, shafting pain to my skull. It was easier to keep my eyes closed.

"Whaa . . . whaa?" Speaking was impossible too. I only succeeded in making unintelligible sounds.

Time was out of sync. I felt myself jostled, hoisted, aimed. With concerted effort, I occasionally lifted my eyelids for the briefest moment. I could form no rational thoughts, could make no logical connective responses.

The pressure slowly eased from my arms, and I felt myself lowered onto something soft. My head teetered forward, sideways, then up. I carefully opened my eyes.

I saw no one, but I heard sounds in the distance. I tried to identify my surroundings. My eyes lighted on a large rectangular shape. A bed. Then on two smaller, darker shapes on the floor at the foot of the bed. Suitcases. I willed my eyes to work. My suitcases! I was back in my hotel room.

Another shape moved into my limited line of vision, approaching me. I felt drool seep from the corners of my mouth and dribble down my chin, my head tilted from side to side. I tried to stop the sickening motion.

The shape came closer, closer. It was the bellboy Donny. No, it was the first man on stage at Fido's. No, wrong again, it was the second man on stage. Finally, it was all of them in one.

My head dropped back, and blackness descended once again.

* * *

I returned to consciousness with a staggering throbbing in my skull. My eyelids felt like they were cemented shut, as if I'd need a crowbar to raise them. My body resisted movement. My muscles screamed their resistance at forced activity. I tried to lift my body up from its lair but found it grounded in quicksand. I finally managed to free my left arm from its suction. But when it moved across the smooth cool surface, it encountered something solid, something sticky, something—

Suddenly I came fully awake. I jerked up in bed, threw off the sheet, and found Donny's naked body lying next to me, with a bleeding chasm yawning obscenely across his throat.

CHAPTE**R** 6

*"Balancing on the high wire of good taste,
the author pokes good-natured fun at himself, his genre, his critics, and even his audi-
ence."*

—*Stokes Moran,
on Thomas Maxwell's* Kiss Me Twice

Blood had saturated the bedding. It had spilled from Donny's neck onto the sheets, the pillowcases, the bedspread. It was on my hands, my arms, my legs and feet.

I vaulted from the bed, aware for the first time that I was naked too. I looked down in horror at Donny's still body, too stunned to comprehend the full impact of what I saw. I acted on my first impulse and ran into the bathroom. I fumbled with the shower controls and got the hot spray going, not even bothering to pull the shower curtain closed. As I frenziedly scrubbed away at Donny's blood, the imponderable questions assaulted my still befuddled brain. What had happened? What was Donny doing in my room? How did he get into my bed? Why was he naked? Why was I naked? And the biggest question of all—who had killed him?

With the last vestiges of Donny's blood dissolving away down the drain, I turned the shower off and stepped out onto the cold tile, grabbing for a convenient towel. Absorbed as I was with the monstrous reality of finding a dead body in my bed, the knock didn't immediately register in my conscious mind. But when it came a second time, I heard it distinctly. And panicked.

Oh my God, the police! It had to be the cops. With a dead body in my bed, who else could it be? Oh Jesus, what do I do?

I wrapped the wet towel around my waist, left the bathroom, and tiptoed to the door. Unfortunately, this was not a hotel that had installed peepholes in its doors.

"Yes?" I cautiously called.

"It's Matthew Hedges. Let me in."

I breathed a relieved sigh. It was not the police. I glanced back at the bloody tableau, considered my chances of disguising or hiding it, then realized it would be fruitless.

Matthew Hedges was not at the top of my hit parade right then, but at least he was somebody I knew. And he had been with me tonight. I thought maybe he could provide some answers to this impossible situation. So even with an incriminating body in my bed, I let him in.

He eased through the narrow opening that I allowed, immediately took in the sight on the bed, and sighed.

"I was afraid something like this would happen. The mood you were in, I should never have left the two of you alone."

"I don't know what you're talking about. What do you mean 'the mood I was in'? The last thing I remember is the two of us sitting in Fido's. Then everything went blank."

Hedges walked over to the bed, looked down at Donny, then lifted the sheet and covered the body.

"I knew you weren't feeling well. You almost passed out. I managed to get you out of Fido's and down to the street where we ran into Donny. He helped me get you back to the hotel. By the time we got up here, you had started yelling and making all sorts of accusations. I left Donny here with you while I went downstairs to get some aspirin."

As if for verification, he extended his right hand and displayed two tablets resting in his palm.

"Donny said he would help get you into bed. I guess you didn't appreciate his kind of help."

Still stupefied by the recent events, I had listened to his fantastic tale without comment. Until then.

"Are you saying you think I killed him?"

"Well, here you are, and there he is." He gestured toward the body.

"You're crazy. What reason would I have for killing a bellboy?"

"Maybe you didn't exactly welcome his advances."

Hedges was painting a sordid picture I didn't like.

"I'm not homosexual."

"I didn't say you were. But Donny was. And maybe he tried to take advantage of your debilitated state."

"Well, what did I cut his throat with—my fingernail?"

He reached under the bed and pulled out a switchblade. I had not noticed it—how had he? It was open and even from across the room I could see the blood on the razor-thin steel.

"That's not mine."

"It's probably Donny's. You know, maybe he got a little rough and—"

"I tell you, we didn't have sex."

"Maybe not, but that's how it'll look to the cops."

I groaned. The cops. I had momentarily put that thought out of my mind; now it came flooding back, with all of its ter-

ror, with all of its finality. I've read enough crime novels to
know how this would look to the police. I sat down on the chair
across from the bed, uncaring that the towel had come open.
Let Matthew Hedges think I was coming on to him too. At this
stage it no longer mattered. At that moment the situation was
beyond my capability to comprehend.

"I guess I better call the cops then. I don't know what else
to do."

Matthew Hedges laid the switchblade down on the tabletop
next to where I sat, reached up and snapped on the lamp.

"I have an idea." He strode over to where Donny's clothes
lay in a heap on the floor, picked up the boy's pants, and rifled
through them. His right hand emerged with a key.

"I have a friend on the hotel staff who can help me get the
body out of here and clean up this mess. That way you'll never
be connected with it."

I stared at him. "Why would you do something like that for
me? Put yourself at risk that way?"

"Well, I feel somehow responsible. If I hadn't left you two
alone up here, Donny never would have come on to you and
he wouldn't have ended up"—he nodded toward the bed—
"there."

I shook my head; it still hurt. "Gimme those aspirin. I need
them now more than ever."

He handed them over; they were beginning to disintegrate.
I popped them in my mouth and swallowed them dry. It was
not a taste I usually liked, but I was too preoccupied to care.

"Let me see if I've got this straight. You're going to take care
of this mess for me. So I can just up and leave and no one will
ever know I was involved. Is that right?"

"Right. I've had to clean up messes for people before. Never this bad, of course, but just as delicate."

"I still don't know why you'd do this. It's not like we're friends or something. Or that you have anything to gain. I certainly can't pay you."

"I don't want anything. Let's just say I'm doing it because I'd hate to see the name Stokes Moran on anything but a mystery review."

My head was hurting too much to argue further, and I was ready to get away from this room, this hotel, and this city. I was constantly conscious that Donny's lifeless body still lay under the sheets of my bed.

What kind of coward would I be to accept Hedges's offer? A free one, I decided shamefully.

"All right," I said. "I'm not thinking too clearly right now, and I'm probably going to regret this. Even though I know I didn't kill him, I'm sure the police would think me doubly guilty by leaving. But I tell you, I'm willing to take the chance. I want to be gone from here, and I don't ever want to come back." I stood up.

"So I may be a fool, but I'll take you up on your offer."

Matthew Hedges smiled. "Then get your things together and go. You can probably catch a red-eye flight out at 6 A.M. That only gives you a couple of hours. I'd suggest you get a move on."

I took his advice. I was packed and out the door within five minutes. I knew it was wrong, even as I was doing it. I was leaving Matthew Hedges literally holding the bag. A body bag. I grimaced. I had never before done anything so reprehensible in my life, but I was powerless to stop myself. I was just too grateful to be free.

CHAPTER 7

"The author knows how to create vivid scenes with very few words, and not one of them is wasted."

—Stokes Moran,
on Bill Crider's Dead on the Island

As soon as the door to Suite Four Twenty-One closed behind me, I felt exposed. Rampant paranoia set in. I thought unseen eyes followed me to the elevator, traveled with me down to the lobby, watched me as I stood waiting for my bill to be processed. I wouldn't look at the desk clerk as he handed me the paperwork to sign, or when he thanked me and wished me good day.

Doubts assailed me. What had I done? I should go back upstairs, call the cops, explain to them what had happened, and take my chances.

Two men lounged in the piano bar, a carpet sweeper pulled his machine back and forth over the floor, a maid emptied ashtrays. I caught their eyes and experienced the panicking sensation that they all knew. It was as if I was wearing a flashing neon sign that screamed *"Murderer."* I had never felt so completely vulnerable, so totally exposed.

I should have checked for Donny's pulse. Maybe he had still been alive. Maybe I could have helped him. No, he had definitely looked dead. Yeah, right. Like with my limited experience with corpses I should know how death looked.

A woman shifted impatiently from foot to foot waiting for the arrival of the elevator to the garage. I held back, not wanting to engage her interest. When the doors separated, she lunged in, with me right behind her. We studiously avoided acknowledging each other on the trip down to the second level. Again, when the doors slid open, she bolted away. Luckily, she headed in a direction opposite to mine.

Go back, I urged. Turn around, be a man. I kept moving forward.

The Buick rental was exactly where I had left it. As I approached, awkwardly fumbling for my car key while attempting to maintain my ponderous grip on the luggage, I heard a noise behind me. Turning, I saw no one. With shaking hands, I inserted the key in the door lock, threw my bags and briefcase across the front seat, and slid behind the steering wheel, hastily pulling the door shut, and immediately clicking the locks in place. My heart was in my throat, my breathing was ragged, and I realized for the first time how extraordinarily frightened I was. A lifetime in prison yawned in front of me if I didn't make it now. I was knowingly leaving the scene of a crime. Even if I were not the killer, my present actions made me at least an accessory. And there were witnesses to my departure—Matthew Hedges, the desk clerk, the people in the lobby. The time I checked out would be notated on my bill. No doubt about it, I was in deep shit. How had I gotten into such a mess?

I started the car.

The drive to the airport took forever. At five o'clock in the morning, I had counted on light traffic. But New Orleans must be a city late to bed and early to rise. Or maybe, like New York, it never sleeps at all. Because, as I turned onto Airline Highway, I got stalled in a bumper-to-bumper crawl. After almost a mile of turtle-like progress, I topped a slight hill and understood the reason for the delay. A fender-bender over in the far left-hand lane had blocked all but the right outside lane, and traffic was being diverted into the one clear artery. Fortunately, I had the Buick already in the free-flowing lane, and I was finally able to ease past the bottleneck.

Once in the clear, I speeded up, making up for lost time. Suddenly, sirens erupted in the distance, and my pulse quickened. Beads of perspiration popped out on my upper lip and at the perimeter of my hairline. Then I belatedly realized that they must be heading for the accident scene.

But the singsong wailing came closer, closer—past the collision site. I thought about prison food and men confined together. Images from *Birdman of Alcatraz* flittered across my memory.

The metronomic blue lights slammed me back to reality. The police car was right behind me, directly in my lane, and approaching fast. I jerked the steering wheel to the right and bumped onto the street's rocky shoulder. The black-and-white zoomed past.

Again, I exhaled my pent-up fear, checked the traffic, and moved out onto the roadway. The remainder of the trip to New Orleans International was uneventful.

Thankful for the express rental check-in, I left the Buick in the parking lot and lugged my baggage across the tarmac to the terminal building. Lee had booked my return passage, but since the length of my stay had been unknown, I had no flight confirmation. I could only hope that at this hour—it was not yet 6 A.M.—I wouldn't encounter a problem getting a seat. I was ready to take any airplane out of New Orleans, even if it was heading to South America.

Luck was with me, however. TWA had a flight departing at six-thirty and I got the last available first-class ticket. The clerk's rueful explanation was holiday travel. I had forgotten how close it was to Christmas. If that thought had entered my head earlier, it would only have heightened my already paranoid anxiety.

I let the clerk check all my baggage. I didn't want to be hampered with luggage if I needed to make a quick run for it. I made a sacred vow never to travel with that much luggage again, no matter what.

With still-lingering apprehension, I made my way through airport security. I decided I would never feel safe around uniforms of any kind again. I arrived at my gate with twenty minutes to spare. The seating area was filling up fast, and I had to take a place in the smoking section, reminding me how desperately I could do with a cigarette. I went in search of a machine, found one, dropped in eight quarters, and pulled the handle for the strongest pack offered—regular Winstons.

No pack dropped into the pick-up slot. I tapped impatiently on the glass. Nothing. I hit it harder. Still nothing. In desperation, I began to pound against the sides. Just then, out of the corner of my eye, I caught sight of an airport security guard walking my way. Oh great, I thought, I make it this far just to get arrested for felonious assault on a vending machine. Stupid, stupid.

I watched the man pass, decided to give up trying to retrieve the cigarettes, and as a parting shot kicked the damn thing. The Winstons dropped.

Drawing the longest drag of my nicotine life, I retreated to the waiting area and remained there until my flight was called. I don't think my heart rate returned to normal or that I started to breathe regularly until the plane was safely in the air somewhere over Mississippi.

C H A PT E R 8

*"With its frosty New England setting and its
pleasant Yuletide cheer, the mystery sets a
lighthearted tone that's just the prescription
for our hectic Christmas pace."*
                                        —*Stokes Moran,*
                    on *Katherine Hall Page's* The Body in the
                                                        Bouillon

Tipton, Connecticut, has been my home now for almost ten years. I like the physical proximity to Manhattan, but even better, I appreciate the emotional and attitudinal light-years' distance from the big city's frenetic pace. Tipton is a quiet hamlet nestled comfortably on the Yessula River. My house is a little farther removed from Broadway than forty-five minutes, but I can usually make it home from Kennedy in under two hours. Today traffic was unaccountably light, my foot was heavy, and I made it in almost half the time.

I pulled into the parking lot of the Minton Animal Clinic at two minutes past four on the day before Christmas Eve. As eager as I was to be home, I was even more anxious to have my dog at home with me. At the time I left Bootsie in Dr. Nancy Minton's safekeeping, I had assumed I would be gone throughout the holiday period and had not paid that much attention to Dr. Nancy's remarks about her change in schedule. I vague-

ly remembered her saying something about the office being
closed Christmas Eve through the day after Christmas. I had
broken all known land speed records getting here before 5 P.M.
because I wanted to take no chance of being without Bootsie
for the next seventy-two hours. Christmas is depressing
enough without having the one you love locked away in a cage.

I shivered against the cold as I climbed out from behind the
wheel of my little 1962 MG. I had purchased the car back sec-
ond-hand in my college days and had spent a fortune on it in
the intervening twenty years, but I had never been able to shift
my desire to any other car. I had found what I wanted and I
was going to stay with it. Even if by now it had cost me the
new purchase price of at least two other automobiles.

Snow was in the air, but not on the ground. I could feel it
against my skin and taste it on my lips. It was great to get back
to weather that was predictable for its time of year. I was even
hopeful of a white Christmas.

I stepped into the much-too-warm vet's waiting room to
the welcome and familiar strains of yelps and barks coming
from the back kennel. I felt home. The incidents in New
Orleans seemed far away and were receding in my memory.

The receptionist's desk was empty. I called out.

"Anybody here?"

No one responded to my query. I walked to the kennel door,
and turned the latch. The first thing I saw as I entered the kennel area was blood on the floor, not just driplets but swashes of
coagulating red ooze.

I felt faint. The images from the hotel room flooded my
brain. Blood, blood everywhere. It was on my hands, my feet.
I smelled it, inhaled it, swallowed it. I sank into red slime.

"Mr. Malachi, are you all right?" Dr. Minton was standing over me. Her long dark hair reached limply toward me. I lay propped against a cage, and she was holding a cold compress to my forehead.

"I must have passed out," I said weakly.

She laughed. "The sight of blood affects some people that way. I'm sorry you had to see it. My assistant went home early, and one of the dogs from this morning's surgery got loose and ripped out his stitches. I chose to attend to his needs before cleaning up his mess. You just happened to walk in at the wrong time."

I started to rise, felt queasy again, and lapsed back against the cage.

"That's fine," she said. "Just stay where you are. You'll have your sea legs back in a minute."

I looked around. Newspapers covered the floor where the blood had been. Dr. Minton saw where I was looking and smiled.

"I didn't have time to clean it up, but I thought it best to get it out of sight."

I swallowed. I was beginning to feel normal again.

"Where's Bootsie?"

"She's out in the run. I didn't expect you back so soon, or I'd have had her washed and combed for you. Do you want to leave her here overnight? I could arrange to let you pick her up in the morning?"

"No way." I was now standing. "I don't want to go another minute without her."

"Well, here's a leash. You can get her out of the run yourself while I finish up in here."

"Thanks, Dr. Nancy."

Always meticulous in every detail, she called after me. "I'll make out a bill, and we can settle up later."

* * *

The gray wood-and-stone structure at the end of the river-fronting cul-de-sac was one of the most welcoming sights of my life, second only to the furry auburn blur I'd seen leaping at me through the wire fence just minutes ago. When I freed Bootsie from her prison, she knocked me over with her enthusiasm, literally. Sprawled as I was on the ground, she attacked me with a friendly vigor only dogs and chess champions can muster. I still had flecks of white foam on my coat sleeves and bits of grass on my pants as evidence of her victorious entrance back into my life. Now she danced eagerly on the front seat, ready to reclaim her rightful territory.

I pulled the car into the driveway and braked to a stop. Bootsie exploded from the car, leaping over me in her eagerness to get out. She ran in circles around the yard, sniffing one favorite spot after another, until the moment I turned the key in the front door, at which time she bolted toward the house, tail wagging mightily. Bootsie felt as I did—being home meant all was right with the world.

I dropped my bags inside the front door, ignored the flashing red light on my answering machine, made a strip-tease march up the stairs, and climbed naked into my bed, pulling the covers over my head. Bootsie settled comfortably at my feet, and the two of us sailed blissfully into safe and welcome sleep.

* * *

I awoke to cold sunshine slicing through my bedroom windows and Bootsie insistently nudging my face. When she realized she had succeeded in rousing me, she started to bark, dancing excitedly between the bed and the door. She had to go and go bad.

I looked at the clock. It was 8 A.M. I couldn't believe it; I had slept for fifteen hours. No wonder the dog was in such a rush.

"Hold on, girl." I promised. "I'll be with you in a minute."

I walked to the closet, couldn't find my good robe, remembered it was still in my luggage, and settled for a summer cotton one that afforded little warmth.

As Bootsie bounded down the stairs ahead of me, I shivered beneath the thin fabric and thought that the house usually wasn't this cold, until I remembered that I had cut the furnace off when I left for New Orleans and in my haste last evening I had failed to turn it back on. Which is the first thing I did after letting Bootsie out the back door. My second chore of the morning was getting the coffee going. And third I checked the messages on my answering machine.

There was only one. "Kyle, call me when you get in." It was my agent, Lee, and she gave no indication of when she had called or what she wanted to talk to me about. I was not yet ready to admit to her my abysmal failure to locate Seymour Severe, let alone share with her the circumstances of my reckless departure from New Orleans. I decided she could wait until after the coffee.

CHAPTER 9

*"People from time to time will ask me just
when it is I make up my mind about a book
I'm reviewing. Sometimes I can tell by reading a few pages what my opinion is likely to
be. Most often, the moment of judgment
comes as I close the book for the last time.
Occasionally, and this is one of those times, I
really don't know how I feel until I sit down
to write the review."*

—Stokes Moran,
on Tony Hillerman's Talking God

Old habits die hard. Stoking a cigarette along with my first
cup of coffee had been the way I had started my days for most
of my adult life. If my trip to New Orleans had accomplished
nothing else, it had reawakened my craving for nicotine.

So, instead of leisurely kicking back with my steaming cup
of coffee, I was frantically exploring all my old hiding places,
hoping that somehow there was still a pack lurking somewhere. In a catchall drawer under the kitchen counter, I finally found one wrinkled Winston. That first drag, stale though it
was, still tingled my toes.

But before I could revel in the sensation, the phone rang.
Let the machine get it, I chided. But I had forgotten I'd set the

damn thing on five rings. So by the third loud interruption of my reverie, I'd had enough.

"Yeah." Normally I don't answer the phone so curtly.

"Kyle? It's Lee. Why so grumpy?"

"I don't know. This morning's not going too well."

"Well, the way you roared at me, it reminded me of the way you were when you were trying to give up smoking." She sounded much too chipper to suit me.

"Yeah. Well." I waved the cigarette smoke away from the phone.

"I called your hotel yesterday morning, and they said you'd checked out. Does that mean you found Severe?"

"No, it means I struck out."

"But you were only down there a little more than twenty-four hours. I thought you'd give it more of a shot than that."

"Yeah. Well." I was not strong on verbal skills this morning.

Lee waited for me to say more. When I did not, she continued. "Kyle, is there something wrong? You don't sound at all like yourself."

"I'm fine, Lee," I lied. "I'm just tired from the trip. Let me call you back a little later." I was ready to hang up, ending one of the shortest conversations between agent and client on record. But Lee was not quite so anxious.

"Well, tell me all that happened. I can't wait to hear."

"I'm afraid you'll have to. I'm sorry, Lee, but I've really got to go."

"Okay, Kyle." She sounded uncertain, but resigned to the mutual dead-end we had reached. "Merry Christmas," she said.

"Merry Christmas," I repeated, without meaning it, and broke the connection. I knew I'd regret my rudeness later. Lee had not only been my agent for the past four years, we'd also become close friends. She didn't deserve this kind of treatment from me, but right at that moment I really didn't care.

I stubbed out the cigarette, remembering only then the pack I'd bought at the airport yesterday, nestling somewhere right now amid the clothes I'd carelessly abandoned on my headlong flight to my bedroom last night.

"Oh well," I mumbled to myself. "At least I'll know where one is next time." I called Bootsie in from outside, and she and I trudged back up the stairs, picking up yesterday's discarded apparel as we went.

I didn't want to think about yesterday. New Orleans, Fido's, the events in my hotel room, my cowardice. Sleep offered the only escape; sometimes, even fifteen hours is not enough. The hell with it all, I was going back to bed.

* * *

This time, it wasn't Bootsie. At first, I thought it was the phone. But, just as I was regaining enough consciousness to correctly identify the sound, the pounding confirmed it. Somebody was at the front door.

The police! They've come to get me. Then, I thought, it serves me right.

With pulses pounding, I struggled into my robe and staggered down the stairs. Bootsie beat me to the door, happy and excited at the prospect of company. I didn't quite share her enthusiasm.

With the most intense feeling of dread I've ever experienced, I opened the door—and found Lee standing on the step.

"Well, it's about time," she said as she breezed past me. I

turned and followed her to the sofa, where she dumped her satchel, and began unfastening her all-weather coat.

"Don't you know it's already after noon and time to be out of bed?"

I almost told her in explicit detail how little it mattered to me, but thought better of the notion.

"Well, aren't you going to say anything?"

I gave her my most withering look and hoped she'd get the message. But with someone as perpetually cheerful as Lee, I doubted that it would take. It didn't.

"Well, all right, Mr. Don't Say a Word, just be that way." She lounged back against the cushions. "I'll just park it right here until you decide to be sociable."

Bootsie had been waiting patiently for Lee's attention. Now she demanded it by climbing halfway into Lee's lap and nuzzling Lee's face. I usually pull Bootsie off guests at this point. But I wasn't feeling at all charitable.

"Well, at least here's someone who's glad to see me." It appeared Lee didn't require my intervention after all. "Yes, that's a girl. What a good girl."

"I'll leave the two of you to your mutual admiration," I said irritably. "I'm going to take a shower." I headed back up the stairs.

"Want any company?" Lee called after me.

"Oh sure," I grumbled under my breath as I topped the last step and turned toward the bathroom.

The steaming water revived me and by the time I had dressed my normally buoyant spirits had returned. When I came back down a few minutes later, I was ready for conversation.

"What the hell are you doing here?" I asked.

Lee looked up from a magazine she was reading, and smiled. "Well, now that you're refreshed from your shower, do you feel a little bit more like talking?"

"No," I said as I walked into the kitchen and started preparing coffee for the second time that day. Lee, right behind me with Bootsie tagging at her heels, began rummaging through the refrigerator.

"Don't you have anything in here to eat?" asked Lee, as she began removing items from the refrigerator and placing them on the kitchen counter.

"I'm not hungry," I grouched as I tried to edge past her, but Bootsie blocked my exit. What I really wanted was a cigarette, but Lee and I had made a pact six months ago. If I gave up smoking, she would too. As far as I knew, she had kept her part of the bargain. So I didn't dare light one up with her around.

"Well, you've got to eat," she said. "Let's see what we can come up with out of all this stuff."

Lee had piled jars of mustard, mayonnaise, relish, pickles, and olives on the counter. She had pulled lettuce, ham, onions, and cheese from the crisper. A couple of lonesome eggs teetered precariously on the counter's edge.

"That stuff's been in there for ages," I complained. "It's probably no good."

"Nonsense." Lee sniffed at the ham and pinched the lettuce. "Looks good to me. Here, make yourself useful." She handed me the eggs. "Boil 'em."

Contrary to what I had said, I was hungry. And the idea of lunch was suddenly quite appealing. Bootsie had taken up a strategic position just out of trampling range but well within lunging distance should any food items find their way to the floor. The dog's a regular vacuum cleaner when it comes to dropped morsels.

For the next few minutes, Lee skillfully chopped lettuce, peeled onions, sliced pickles and olives, and grated cheese. She left me the easy tasks, such as cleaning up her messes and gulping a sip of coffee when I could manage it.

"Where's the bread?"

"It's in the freezer."

"Freezer! What's it doing in the freezer?"

"I don't eat much bread."

Lee opened the freezer door, shoved a few things around, then pulled out a frozen French loaf. She tore the plastic wrapping away from it and handed the bread to me. "Stick this in the microwave."

"The whole thing?"

"Yes, the whole thing. What are you—some kind of miser?"

"I told you, I don't eat much bread."

"No wonder you're so thin."

A domesticated Lee Holland was something I'd never expected. I didn't think she knew what a kitchen was, let alone be able to master the finer art of cooking. But here she was, making a shambles out of my kitchen, and doing it very capably.

I smiled. Watching Lee attack the shell of a hard-boiled egg, I realized what an extraordinarily attractive woman she was. Standing there working over the sink, barefooted (she must have discarded her shoes along with her coat), in simple tan slacks and blouse, I had never before found her so alluring. Nor had I ever noticed how truly tiny she was. She didn't stand much over five feet, and I doubted if she even weighed a full hundred pounds. All these years, all those business lunches, and I was suddenly seeing her for the first time. Her thick dark hair shimmered when she moved.

"Here, cut these up." She handed me the newly naked eggs.

"Do you have any idea what you're making?"

She smiled. "Besides a mess you mean?"

"Yes, besides a mess?"

"You'll just have to wait and see." She lifted the bread out of the microwave. She spread butter and garlic salt on it, then handed it to me. "Now, pop it in the oven for a few minutes.

"In the broiler," she added when I started to put it in the wrong place.

"Yes, Julia Child."

The meal, when it was completed, was surprisingly good. Lee had thrown everything together, added some tuna, and turned it into a delicious if somewhat unusual salad. The garlic bread topped it all off.

I stepped back from the counter. We had eaten standing up, right where we had prepared the food, rejecting the more obvious convenience of the stools around the breakfast bar and opting instead for the companionable informality of munching from the counter top.

"Does what we just ate have a name?" I asked, setting my plate gingerly into the sink.

"Just call it Chef's Surprise."

"It was certainly that," I concurred.

"Now that I've fed you," Lee smiled, "and jollied you," she winked, "into a better mood"—then her tone turned serious—"will you please tell me what's wrong?"

Which I did.

* * *

"Write the review."

"What?"

"Write the review."

It had taken almost half an hour for me to go through the entire story for Lee. She had sat on the sofa, legs propped up on the coffee table, listening intently, never interrupting, never asking questions, never registering any sign of reaction. I had expected outrage, or shock, or, at the very least, sympathetic clucking. So her words, when she finally did speak, caught me by surprise.

"What do you mean, write the review?"

"It's a murder mystery, isn't it? Do what you do best. Review it."

I couldn't believe her total lack of response, her emotional detachment, her seeming disinterest. It was as if she were just giving me an ordinary assignment.

I was getting angry. "Did you hear anything I said? I'm talking real life here. I'm not making this up. This is not fiction."

Lee stood up and walked over to the front window, parted the draperies, and gazed out into the cold Connecticut twilight. After a minute, she turned back toward me.

"I know that. I just think there're some things you're missing here. Probably because you're too close to the situation to see it objectively." She headed off toward the kitchen, Bootsie following hopefully at her heels. "I'm going to make some coffee. You—write the review."

* * *

It took me two hours to write the review, but less than half that to see what Lee was driving at. I had been too close, too personally involved, to be an objective observer. All those times that I had criticized mysteries when I felt the characters had behaved stupidly or the detectives had ignored obvious clues now came back to taunt me. Things aren't quite so easy to read in real life.

I hit the print key on my PC, got up from the desk, stretched, then went in search of Lee. I found her in the kitchen, sitting at the bar, cradling a cup of coffee in her hands, Bootsie sprawled in a dead sleep at her feet. She looked up at my entrance.

"Finished?"

"Yeah." I walked to the refrigerator, opened it, and took out a can of soda. I popped the top and took a big gulp. As always, that first swallow brought an involuntary hiccough.

"Excuse you," said Lee, smiling.

I came around the bar and sat next to her, took another big sip, and placed the soda on the counter.

"Well?" she asked.

I turned and looked her squarely in the eyes. "I'm giving up mystery writing."

"Why?"

"Because it's not as simple as I thought. It takes more than just knowing how it's done, more than just understanding the mechanics, to get it right."

I shifted my gaze away from her, but she grabbed my shoulders and turned me back toward her.

"All right, tell me all about it."

I shook my head. "I can't believe how stupid, how boneheadedly stupid I was. Or am. I was a complete fool. I'm not even sure I'm fit to do reviews."

"Don't you think you may be a tad overreacting?"

"No I don't." I left the stool, walked over to the window, and looked out into the backyard, seeing the winter-killed grass and leafless trees. On the far side of the fence, I spied my next-door neighbor, Nolan James, walking toward his utility shed. Nolan always collects my mail for me whenever I'm out of town for more than a couple of days. Damn, I thought, I guess Nolan's wondering why I haven't yet been over. But at the moment, I dreaded the prospect of neighborly chitchat and decided the mail would just have to wait. Suddenly Bootsie nudged my hand, then turned a complete circle toward the door. I opened it and let her out. I turned back to Lee.

"When I think of how gullible, how totally ridiculous I was, it makes me so . . . so . . . "

"Mad?" Lee smiled.

"Yes. And angry, furious, outraged. Find the thesaurus, I need some more words."

Lee laughed. "I'm glad you're angry. It shows you're human."

I sat down next to her again. "But how did you know? I was blind to the whole thing, but you saw through it right away. Why?"

"The story you told just didn't hold water. It didn't make sense. Plus, I thought it impossible that you'd be in New Orleans for less than twenty-four hours and get mixed up in murder. Now twenty-four days, possibly; twenty-four hours, no."

"You saw it. Why couldn't I see it?"

"Because it didn't happen to me. It happened to you. And I

had the advantage of hearing it. It played out in my mind as you were telling it just as if I were reading a book or watching a movie. And I just didn't buy it."

"The willing suspension of disbelief." How many times had I listed that as the essential element to any successful mystery novel. I shook my head.

"Exactly," Lee agreed. "But it was more than that too. The guy you described—what was his name? Matty?"

"Yes, Matty Hedges."

"Dressed all in white, showing up everywhere you went, knowing things he couldn't have known. It was just too pat, too—"

"Hokey," I finished for her.

"Yes, that too. But I was going to say, too scripted."

"I came to the same conclusion in my review. In fact, I think I even felt it while it was happening. I just couldn't understand why, so I guess I accepted it without really analyzing it."

Lee stood up, placed her hands on my shoulders, and began rubbing my back. "You're not supposed to analyze life; you've got to live it. I think you've been holed up here too long, lost in a fictional world of drug pushers, serial killers, and cozy murderers. It hasn't prepared you for the real world."

"You want to read what I wrote. It's probably my last review."

"I'll read it later. It accomplished what I wanted. You finally understand what was done to you."

"Yes," I admitted. I remembered the terror I'd felt, the shame of my cowardice, the guilt of my actions. "I was turned into the world's biggest sap. What a joke I must have been. The big-shot mystery reviewer. Oh, what a laugh they must have had."

I twisted my neck to meet Lee's eyes. "But you know the thing that galls me most. You'd think as a mystery reader I'd have realized that not all dead bodies are necessarily dead bodies."

"But you had no way of knowing that Donny was playing possum."

"I should have checked. If I had been reading it, instead of living it, I would have suspected something along those lines. But, stupid me, I fell so easily into their trap. Every time I think about what a dunce I was not to even check for a pulse it just makes me so mad."

Lee stopped the back rub, rested her head on my shoulder, and whispered in my ear.

"Good. Now that you understand, don't you think it's time to get even?"

* * *

Lee outlined her plan to me in less than twenty minutes. She had worked it out while I had been writing the review, she told me. Lee did not have to employ much persuasion—I bought into it immediately. The two of us ironed out the details over the next couple of hours.

When we had just about finalized everything to our mutual satisfaction, Lee made a couple of phone calls while I considered the untenable situation I'd inexplicably gotten myself into.

"There's still one thing I can't figure," I said, after she'd hung up the phone for the last time.

"What's that?"

"Why? Why would they go to so much trouble, plot so elaborate a hoax, just to get rid of me? I could have stayed in New Orleans for weeks and never gotten close to Severe."

"You have to remember this guy's a creative genius. I think it's a tribute to your talent, your reputation, that he concocted this scheme and enlisted these people just to challenge you."

I laughed. "I think that's a lot of bullshit. But no matter, I quite obviously failed the test. I'm sure he viewed me as a major disappointment." I heard a scratch at the back door. I had forgotten Bootsie was outside. Normally I don't leave her out for more than a few minutes without checking on her. But it had been—I looked at my watch—almost three hours! I couldn't believe it; I had never been that careless before. The fact I had other matters weighing on my mind was no excuse. You never know what can happen to an animal even inside a fenced backyard. Here was more guilt for me to absorb.

I got off the stool and went to let Bootsie in. The extended time outdoors must have been to her liking, because she bounded into the room with the energy and expectation of a dog replenished by fresh air and temporary freedom from human constraints. As usual, she headed straight for the bottom cabinet that held her Milk-Bones, demanding her customary reward for having responsibly taken care of business. Unlike me with Severe, I didn't disappoint her.

"I don't know that I'd agree," Lee answered my last remark. "I think you probably behaved just as he expected. Look at it this way. To him, you were only a character in his story, and you followed the story line beautifully. I'm sure he's quite pleased with your performance."

"Yeah. I'll bet he nominates me for an Oscar." I retook my seat at the bar.

"Edgar, Kyle. Remember your genre."

"Oh yes, right. We must be consistent."

Lee smiled. "Now you're sounding more like your old sarcastic self. You had me worried."

"Can't keep a good man down for long." I stood up."I'm famished. Whaddaya say we go out to eat."

"Kyle, it's Christmas Eve. We'll be mobbed."

"I don't care. I feel like celebrating." I took Lee by the elbows and lifted her from the stool. "Get your coat. I want to get back and get into bed early." Did Lee blush? No, that couldn't be right; I must have been mistaken. "We've got a big day ahead of us tomorrow."

And I didn't mean Christmas.

CHAPTER 10

*"From here on out, no discussion of serious
mystery novelists can fail to include her
name."*

—*Stokes Moran,
on Sharyn McCrumb's* The Hangman's
Beautiful Daughter

Lee was right. We were mobbed. At a Wendy's no less. Finally, after two hours and a dozen napkins, I inserted the key in my front door, twisted it open, and was immediately assaulted by seventy pounds of frenzied Irish setter.

"Is she always that happy to see you?" Lee asked, closing the door behind us while I tried to restrain Bootsie from sharing her energetic welcome with Lee as well.

"Yes," I gasped. "It doesn't matter whether I'm gone two hours or two weeks, it's always the same."

Bootsie was calming down, so I released her. She leaped on Lee, not with the same force with which she'd greeted me, but still with enough momentum to cause Lee to stagger under the blow.

"Down," I ordered in my sternest voice.

Bootsie obeyed, but her enthusiasm was undiminished. Her tail flailed the air.

"Kyle, if only I had her energy." Lee laughed.

"Yeah, we could bottle it and make a fortune," I agreed. "I'm going to take her into the kitchen and feed her. That'll keep her out of our hair for a while. If she's got one thing greater than her energy, it's her appetite."

Bootsie and I trotted off together toward the kitchen while Lee slipped off her coat. When I returned a few minutes later, Lee was sitting on the couch, legs tucked under her. I settled next to her.

"Would you like a fire?" I asked.

"That would be nice." Lee smiled, then added, "Nice and romantic."

"Romantic?" I scoffed. I stood, walked over to the fireplace, picked up a few sticks of kindling, and began making the preparations. I talked as I worked.

"You've been reading too many of those stupid romance novels. By those equally stupid romance novelists you handle."

Lee bristled. "They are not stupid. Just because you don't happen to have a romantic bone in your body doesn't mean other people don't."

She seemed angrier than my gibes warranted. "Hey, I didn't mean to upset you."

"You didn't upset me." Lee glared at me, giving lie to her words. "Romance novels fill a need in a lot of people's lives—a lot of lonely people. Plus," her tone brightened, "they make a lot of money. And a hefty percentage of it goes to me."

"Well, I'm all for free enterprise," I said.

"It seems to me you have a very selective memory," Lee chided. "Don't I remember you giving a rave review to Natasha Cooper?"

"Yeah, for *Poison Flowers*. I loved the way the author handled the dual personality of her main character."

Lee smiled smugly. "Well, it might surprise you to learn that Natasha Cooper is really Daphne Wright, a romance novelist."

I returned to the sofa, having succeeded in getting two fires blazing, one in the hearth and the other in Lee.

"And," Lee continued, "don't forget Agatha Christie."

My only comment this time was "Yes." I knew where Lee was heading, so at this moment I didn't bother reminding her that Agatha Christie was one of my all-time favorite mystery writers.

"Christie wrote romances under the name Mary Westmacott."

"Okay," I admitted. "I spoke without thinking."

"You certainly did," Lee agreed. "And how would you categorize Daphne du Maurier, Mary Stewart, Phyllis Whitney, and Velda Johnston?"

Lee paused for my answer. I didn't disappoint her.

"Romantic suspense."

"Aha." Lee jumped on my response. "Romantic suspense, huh?" She jabbed me in the ribs. "Romantic, romantic, romantic!"

By this time, we were both laughing. I admitted my narrow-minded stupidity, but Lee still had a serious point to make.

"Good writers are good writers, Kyle, whether they are men or women, whether they write mysteries or romances or Westerns, whether they produce novels or short stories, plays or poetry. Or reviews. You know that. Your reviews reflect that."

"You're right," I admitted. And she was. When I sit down to write a review, I make it a point to try to remove as much personal bias as possible from my assessment of the book. It's not always easy, but it's the only fair thing to do. Every mystery novel should be judged on its own merits, its own unique qualities. That's the premise I've always tried to follow in my mystery reviewing. Books shouldn't suffer just because the reviewer is having a bad day, or doesn't particularly care for the subject matter, or is angry over something else entirely. And all books should be reviewed on the basis of what the author actually wrote, not what the reviewer wishes had been written.

"This isn't like you at all, Kyle," Lee chastised. "You're the most objective and balanced reviewer I've ever come across. That's why you have such an outstanding reputation."

I shrugged. "Luckily, I write my opinions and normally don't talk them. It's when I speak without thinking that I usually get into trouble." I laughed. "But the odd thing is, this isn't really my opinion. I can assure you I don't feel any animosity toward romance writers. I don't know why I said what I did."

"Just promise me one thing," Lee said. "Please don't dismiss anyone's talent just because you might not happen to appreciate their particular field of endeavor."

Justifiably chastened, I nodded agreement. "You're absolutely right," I said, and then added, "I'm sorry."

Those two words seemed to mollify Lee, who now appeared totally relaxed—a typical picture of the calm after the storm. I had never before seen her become so perturbed over any offhand remark, but I had really stumbled into a hornet's nest this time. Maybe I had treaded too near her livelihood.

"Speaking of money," I said, forgetting for the moment that Lee couldn't read my thoughts and also wanting to shift the conversation back to less controversial territory, "as badly as I need that twenty-five thousand, I'm having second thoughts about your plan."

This set Lee off again.

"Kyle, why?" she demanded.

"Suppose Donny really is dead. I could be heading into real trouble."

"How many times do I have to tell you—Donny is not dead," Lee asserted. "And on the one chance in a million that he is, our plan covers that possibility too."

I nodded. "But why do we have to go to such complicated extremes? We know where he is. Why don't we just go and confront him?"

Lee stood up, walked over, and stopped in front of the fire. "We've been over that," she said, her back still facing me. She picked up the poker and began prodding the burning logs. Then, she turned. "You announced your arrival once, and look what happened. Do you think it would be any different the second time? We have to catch them by surprise."

"Okay, I understand that, but . . ." My voice trailed off.

"But what?" Lee insisted.

I got up from the couch and joined Lee by the fire. I turned my head and caught the glimmering firelight reflected in her eyes.

"What if Donny's dead?" I repeated.

Lee started to say something, stopped. The cast to her eyes changed, and she smiled.

"There's someone I know who lives in New Orleans," she said softly. "A client. I'll give her a call and see if she can help get you an answer."

She walked over to the phone.

"A client?" I queried as she placed the call. Then, unable to resist the temptation, I added,"One of those romance writers, I bet?"

Lee shot me a reproving look. "As a matter of fact," she began, but her immediate "hello" forestalled any further explanation.

While Lee was making her New Orleans connection, I wandered into the kitchen. Bootsie was lying on the floor in front of her untouched food. Out of long habit, she growled at my approach.

"Guarding that dog chow, huh?" I smiled. "Well, don't worry, girl. I'm not going to bother it."

I took a Coke Classic from the refrigerator, popped the top, and sipped it gingerly, this time avoiding the inevitable burp. I walked with the moisture-dripping red-and-white can back into the living room. Lee was just replacing the phone in its cradle as I entered.

"Everything's set," she said. "We should know in a couple of hours about Donny's fate."

"And mine as well," I added morosely.

* * *

It was after midnight when the call finally came. Lee had put some Christmas music on the stereo, and we had spent a pleasant evening talking about past holiday experiences. Around eleven-thirty the conversation had died a natural death, and I had not realized I had nodded off until the phone rang.

I listened in half-wakefulness to Lee's responses, making little sense out of the "uh-huhs" and the "I sees." Finally I heard the longed-for "good-bye."

"Kyle." Lee was shaking me. "Kyle, wake up."

"I'm awake," I said.

"Then open your eyes."

"Why?"

"Kyle, don't be like that."

"I can hear you just as well with my eyes shut as I can with them open." But I opened my eyes all the same. "Okay, what is it?"

"I think it's good news," Lee said. "At least it's half-and-half."

"Well, tell me, dammit." I was now fully alert.

"Okay, first there's been nothing in the newspapers. Not a word." Lee paused, then added, "But this is the clincher. There's been no police report of a homicide that even comes close to matching up."

"That's great." I leaped from the couch, stumbling over Bootsie in the process, who had sometime during my dozing arranged herself around my feet. "That means Donny's alive." I grabbed Lee and crushed her in my embrace, lifting her off her feet and whirling her around in the air. "And it also means I didn't kill anybody. I'm in the clear. To hell with New Orleans, to hell with Seymour Severe, to hell even with the twenty-five grand, nothing in this world's getting me back there. I'm home free." I kissed her full on the lips.

"Not necessarily." Lee squeaked out the words.

"What do you mean?" I demanded. I set Lee back down on the floor and released her from my hold.

"Donny's not at the hotel."

I shrugged. "So, he probably just took the night off, don't you think? After all, he told me he'd been working double shifts."

Lee shook her head. "Kyle, you don't understand. Donny hasn't been seen at the hotel in two days. Nobody there knows where he is."

"You don't mean—"

She nodded. "It seems Donny's disappeared."

CHAPTER 11

*"Just when you think you have it figured out,
the author makes an unexpected turn and
startles you with his next surprise."*
—Stokes Moran,
on Loren D. Estleman's Lady Yesterday

We were on the road by nine-thirty the next morning.
Christmas morning. It surely didn't seem like Christmas. Even
though I live alone, and don't have any family, I still always try
to celebrate the holiday. Get a tree. Buy some presents. Watch
classic Christmas movies on TV, like *Miracle on 34th Street* and
Christmas in Connecticut. But this year I had done nothing.
With all the preoccupation surrounding my pursuit of Seymour
Severe, I'd let the season pass me by.

Lee turned onto Route 107 and headed toward New York.
She was behind the wheel of her Land Rover, with me in the
front seat beside her, and the dog sprawled out in the back.
Bootsie would not be staying with Dr. Nancy this time out. She
was going to have a little adventure of her own.

Traffic was light. As we passed row after row of prefabricat-
ed houses, one looking much like its neighbor, I could imagine
the family scenes currently playing themselves out. Kids eagerly opening and, almost as quickly, destroying their new toys,
dads exhausted from their previous night's labors, moms

already in the kitchens hard at work on Christmas dinner. The way it used to be for me, the way it was no more.

Christmas is the only time of the year when I truly regret the absence of a family. My mother died of cancer when I was in college. My father lived with the loss for barely a year before he decided the pain was too unbearable and took his own life. I had no brothers or sisters, no aunts or uncles. Barely in my twenties, I suddenly felt alone, isolated, abandoned.

It's hard to get anybody to understand how a twenty-one-year-old man can be an orphan. For some reason a grown man just doesn't get the same sympathy or comfort a ten-year-old would get under the same circumstances. But that doesn't mean the pain is not just as great, the sense of abandonment as intense, the feeling of isolation as fierce, the hurt of separation as real. I wasn't prepared for the aloneness. I had no support group to fall back on. In my senior year in college, I realized I had no family, no close friends, no one to rely on except myself. I think that revelation determined the next two decades of my life.

Because here I was—almost forty years of age—in just about the same shape I'd been in back then. Still without family, still without any close friends. I had chosen my life, no doubt about that. I couldn't blame anyone but myself. It was the way I had thought I wanted it. I had even fashioned a career where no other person was needed.

Reading is a solitary endeavor. So is writing. Life as a mystery reviewer had ensured I would remain alone, untouched, unapproachable. Some days I had no human contact at all, just Bootsie to keep me company. Other days I saw and spoke only to grocery store clerks or gas station attendants. Lee was

the only permanent human fixture in my life, and my lifeline
to her was basically the telephone.

"Hey, how about rejoining the living?" Lee spoke.

"What?"

"I said it's about time you came back from wherever it was
you'd gone."

"I was just thinking."

"Well, think out loud. I'm getting bored with no conversation."

"Talk to Bootsie."

"Bootsie's asleep. And anyway I don't think she much cares
what I have to say."

"And you think I do?"

Lee smiled. "Good. I'm always reassured by your sarcasm.
I know then that we're communicating."

"You call this communicating?"

Lee nodded her head. "It's better than silence."

She had me there. It got me to wondering again. Had I lost
the art of communication? Had somewhere along the line my
personal skills wasted away?

I stayed vocal the rest of the trip into Manhattan, talking
movies and mysteries and anything else that came to mind. I
owed it to Lee; more than that I owed it to myself.

* * *

Manhattan Industrial Graphics is located in a converted ware-
house on the Lower West Side, just a couple of blocks from the
river, at 51 John Street. The ten-foot-tall sign—MIG 51—on
the building's dirty gray exterior signaled our arrival.

Lee pulled to the curb, stopping in a clearly marked

"Loading Zone—Absolutely No Parking." I doubted there'd be much loading or unloading on Christmas Day, but the idea of even a minor legal infraction bothered me. I said as much to Lee, who just grinned, and added, "Considering what the two of us are going to be involved in over the next few days, I wouldn't worry about it." And then, to underscore her dismissal of my objection, she killed the motor.

The trip into the city had been relatively uneventful, and we had made very good progress. Lee avoided the expressways as much as possible and stuck to the surface streets. Even with that, it had taken us only a little over an hour total driving time.

Bootsie stirred in the backseat, coming awake for the first time since our departure. I snapped the leash onto her collar and looped it securely around my right hand. Even with no potential four-wheeled deathtraps in sight, I wasn't about to take any chances.

Lee and I released our seat belts and opened our doors. Bootsie jumped over the seat and pulled me out into a jarringly cold New York morning. It had not seemed this cold when we left Tipton. Maybe it was our proximity to the Hudson River, but the wind—approximating gale force intensity—peppered the skin with sharp icy pinpricks.

Bootsie loved it. She took a minute to sniff the area, rejecting several spots until she located a few scrawny shoots of grass between the sidewalk and the gutter. Once finished with her fastidious rituals, she suddenly decided it was time to play, and fought against my lead. Lee, already sheltering in the relative comfort of the doorway toward which I was making little headway, smiled smugly. Normally Bootsie wins out in tugs-of-war like this, but not today. I was too cold and too preoccupied with other constraints to indulge her exercise whim at this particular moment. Besides we all had business to conduct.

Finally Bootsie and I joined Lee, and she touched the button beside the glass-fronted door. A few seconds later the lock clicked open. We were expected, a result of one of last night's phone calls. Lee pushed against the door, holding it open while I unceremoniously shoved Bootsie inside the building.

Lee led the way down a dimly lighted corridor. Bootsie, no longer resisting, trotted eagerly at my side. We entered an elevator, and Lee punched the button marked "3." A slight whirring noise gave the only indication of movement. Momentarily the doors parted, and we stepped out into a brightly illuminated loft.

"Mark?" Lee called. There was no answer.

The room was large, running the entire length of the building, but even so, the only way to describe it was cluttered. Computers sat atop desks; metal shelves filled with a variety of bizarre and unidentified items reached almost to the ceiling; boxes littered the floor. We threaded our way through and around this confusion, with Lee calling Mark's name again and again.

We emerged from the maze into a fairly open space, and almost immediately I heard a low growl start deep in Bootsie's throat. Then Lee screamed. She turned and hid her face against my chest. I gazed over her head to the scene beyond.

A man lay dead on the tile floor, his neck ravaged by some terrible instrument, blood spilling from the wound. I felt faint. It was New Orleans all over again. I closed my eyes to shut out the awful sight, seeing nothing but waves of blood behind my lids. Then I felt Lee shaking against me. At first I thought she was sobbing, until I heard the laughter. I opened my eyes. The man was rising from the floor, and he too was laughing. Pretty soon so was I.

"Oh, Mark," Lee gasped between laughs. "You were just wonderful. No wonder poor Kyle was so completely fooled in New Orleans. If I hadn't known what to expect, I'd have thought for sure you were dead."

I stared at Lee. "You were in on this?"

"Of course," Mark answered for her. "Who do you think set it up?"

"You could have told me," I protested petulantly, still glaring at Lee.

She turned serious. "No, that was the one thing I couldn't do."

Mark was pulling off the gory makeup. "Lee wanted you to be surprised. She wanted you to understand what was done to you, and also how it was done."

"You know?"

He nodded.

"Everything?" I persisted.

He nodded again.

Lee cupped my face in her hands. "Kyle, don't be angry. I had to tell him. So he can help."

Mark Crews, as Lee had informed me the previous evening, owned MIG 51. A former makeup artist for Columbia Pictures, Mark had turned a computer affinity into a full-time and highly profitable occupation, merging his motion picture expertise with the latest technological miracles. According to Lee, he was nothing short of a genius. From what I had seen already, I couldn't dispute it.

With only putty marks remaining around his face, I had an opportunity to fully appraise Mark for the first time. He was an angular man, extremely tall and gangly. He reminded me of the early Jimmy Stewart, with his prominent Adam's apple, high cheekbones, and long and bony fingers, the last noted as we belatedly shook hands. He was clean-shaven, and his hair was combed back from his forehead. The only characteristic preventing him from being the young Stewart's doppelganger was the ponytail, neatly tied behind his head.

Now that the playacting was over, Mark was eager to proceed. "I've got everything ready," he told Lee. "Just like you asked for."

Mark sat before his computer terminal and motioned for us to come around behind him. Bootsie settled comfortably at my feet, restful now that the perceived danger had passed. I looked at Lee standing over Mark and wondered, as I had last night, what kind of relationship could get a man to give up his Christmas holiday. Not to mention the involved theatrics of a few minutes ago. Either they were very good friends, or I didn't want to know.

"Kyle." Mark was addressing me, so I refocused my thinking on the matter at hand. "You'll see as I scroll through these screens"—he pressed a key and the color monitor changed graphics— "that we have a variety of facial features—hair, lips, chins, foreheads—from which to choose. When you see one you think is right, we'll save that option and continue to the next. Hopefully, when we finish the sequence, we'll have something pretty close to the real thing."

We started with the eyes.

For the next three and a half hours, Mark set a grueling pace. He led me through a painstaking yet fascinating reconstruction. Slowly the face that emerged on screen became recognizable. Finally, when we were finished, the image on the computer matched my memory exactly—it *was* Donny. The boy I'd supposedly murdered.

Throughout the long process, Lee had remained patiently silent. Now, hearing me sign off on the last change and declare the picture complete, she spoke as Mark triumphantly hit the "Save" key.

"I'm starved. Let's see if we can't find someplace around here that'll serve us a Christmas dinner."

Leaving Bootsie happily asleep, after assurances from both Mark and Lee that she would do just fine unsupervised, we drove in Lee's Land Rover into nearby Chinatown. Luck was with us, and we found an open restaurant with no difficulty at all. I guess the Chinese are not big Christmas observers because I noticed a good bit of activity in Chinatown, with a number of stores and restaurants conducting business. Over sweet-and-sour pork, we discussed the next step in our plan.

"Now that we have the composite of the boy," Mark explained, "I can attach it to a body similar in size and shape to his that I already have stored in the computer's memory." Mark sounded a little like Dr. Frankenstein describing the assemblage of his monster. "Then I can get the computer to show him in a variety of poses and close-ups."

"And you can print those out just like photographs?" Lee asked.

"That's right. Just like Kodak."

"Amazing," I said.

"But I think the most persuasive shot will be the family portrait, with the two of you with the boy."

OTHERWISE KNOWN AS MURDER

"And don't forget Bootsie," Lee added. The inclusion of the family dog in the picture, or so Lee had argued the night before, would be the one little detail that would give unquestioning authenticity to our claim.

"Yes, the idea of adding Bootsie to the photograph is a real masterstroke," Mark unknowingly echoed. "I don't think anyone will give your story a second thought once you pull out that picture."

Lee's smiling eyes met mine, and I could read the *I told you so* lurking teasingly behind the violet irises.

"But before we can work on the all-American family," Mark said, "we have to get you ready." He was looking at me.

"What do you mean?" I asked.

"Lee and Bootsie are fine as they are. After all, no one knows what they look like. But you're known, you've been seen. So, we have to change you up."

"Change me up how?" I wasn't sure I wanted changing.

"Oh, a little of this and a little of that," Mark commented mysteriously. "Come on, if we're ready to go, I'll show you."

I covered the check with two twenties, which translated into a substantial tip for our waiter (but what the hell, I thought, it's Christmas), and we left the restaurant.

Lee drove us back to MIG 51, parking in the same illegal spot as before. This time, I said nothing.

Mark told Lee to go upstairs and wait with Bootsie while he gave me an "overhauling." His word, not mine.

We watched the elevator close behind Lee, whose last glimpse sent me a thumbs-up sign, then Mark opened a nearby door and we descended to the basement.

"I didn't want Lee watching your transformation," Mark

said as we walked down a carpeted corridor. "I'd rather see her reaction to the finished product." He made me sound like some kind of commodity. He stopped at an open door near the end of the hallway, flipped a switch, and ushered me into a small room that had the appearance of a dentist's office. There was this chair, and these strange-looking tools—

I guess my face must have communicated my dismay. "Don't worry," Mark offered reassuringly. "This won't hurt a bit. Now sit."

"What won't hurt?" I asked, still experiencing some trepidation, even as I followed Mark's command and sat.

"Makeup is an art," Mark commented, without responding to my last question. "Most people, when they try to disguise themselves, usually do it outrageously, and end up giving themselves away. Subtlety is really the key." He stood behind me and placed a towel around my neck. Suddenly I heard a hum.

I twisted in the chair to see what he was doing. "Hey, what is that?"

He held the device out for my inspection. "What does it look like?" he asked.

"It looks like a comb."

"It is a comb," he said, as he gripped my shoulders and turned me back toward the front. "Now stop worrying."

"I'd worry less if you'd tell me what you're doing."

"Okay," he said, as he began to run the electric comb through my hair. "One of your most prominent features, and one of the easiest to alter, is your hair. It's very thick. So all I'm doing is thinning it."

"So that's not a comb."

OTHERWISE KNOWN AS MURDER

"Not exactly, no. It's a cutter." Mark pulled the comb out of my hair and brought it within my vision so I could inspect it more closely. "See how far apart the teeth are? And between the teeth the tiny blades?"

"Yes."

"Well, that allows me to thin the hair without affecting the length." He started combing again. "When I'm finished, you will look considerably different, and I really won't have done that much."

For the next few minutes, Mark worked in silence. He had been quite patient with me, and, after all, I was supposedly a willing participant in all this. So I decided not to question him any further.

"Done." The humming stopped, and Mark placed the comb on a table next to my chair and pulled the towel away from my neck. Hair—formerly my hair, and a lot of it—cascaded to the floor.

"Can I see?" The room, unlike a barbershop, had no mirrors on the walls. But it had everything else, including a porcelain sink.

"Not yet. Wait for the full effect."

Mark snapped something under the chair and leaned me carefully back against the sink. He then shampooed and rinsed my hair. At least that's what I assumed he was doing. After he repeated the process three times, I wasn't so sure.

He pushed me up to a full sitting position, took out a blow dryer, and brushed my hair dry. He reached under the table and brought out a spray bottle that he placed in my hand.

"I want you to use that stuff every day," he said.

"What is it?"

"Basically, it's hair spray."

"Basically?"

"Well, it has a little coloring in it too." He then showed me another bottle he promised would remove the coloring when the time came. He said he'd put everything I needed in a sack I could take with me.

Mark lifted the first bottle out of my hand and sprayed some of the contents into my hair. He then brushed my hair back from my forehead, contrary to my normal style. Mark moved to my side, cocked his head, and appraised his handiwork. He then opened a drawer in the table and handed me a mirror.

"Okay, you can look."

By this time, I wasn't sure I wanted to. But I slowly turned the glass to face me anyway, not quite prepared for the almost stranger looking back at me. I smiled; the image smiled back. It was me, all right, but what a change. I had always prided myself on my boyish appearance; now I looked middle-aged.

Mark had accomplished an amazing metamorphosis. My sandy-blond hair was now dark brown. And thin. Combing the hair back against my scalp gave the unmistakable impression of a receding hairline. Male pattern baldness was my only thought.

"Well?" Mark asked.

My self-absorption had been so great that I had forgotten to speak.

"It's . . . different," I offered lamely.

"You've got that right."

At that instant, I realized Lee and I were actually going to do it, that we really could pull off the impossible. And, just as suddenly, I approved of all Mark had done.

"It's great," I said. "I don't think even I would have recognized me."

Mark seemed pleased. "Don't get too carried away. Hold your final judgment until we've finished. There are still more surprises to come."

* * *

"Kyle? Kyle, is that you?"

Lee's voice held a note of stunned incredulity. Almost four hours had passed since she'd last seen me, and I could understand her consternation. Just minutes ago, looking at myself in the full-length mirror in Mark's residential quarters on the second floor, I had experienced much the same sensation. My change in hairstyle was nothing compared to the overall effect.

After Mark had completed the first stage of my makeover, he had next moved to alter the set of my jaw. He had labored diligently for quite a while crafting a mouthpiece out of some kind of pliable plastic. While he worked on this feature, I really had felt like I was in the dentist's chair. I had to hold my mouth open while he took measurements and fittings.

"Boxers now use this same material to protect their teeth and tongue during a fight," Mark said, more talkative at this stage than he had been earlier. "All I'm doing is taking the concept one step further.

"Over the past fifteen years, I guess I've done makeup for close to a hundred TV shows and movies. I just wish Poliform" (that was the name of the product) "had been available when I first started in the business. It would have made life so much simpler."

"Yuk." Some of that miracle product had brushed against the back of my tongue.

"I know. Right now it tastes horrible. But when it hardens—and that's why I'm working so fast, it sets quick—it won't have any taste at all.

"You'd be surprised at the number of famous faces I've worked on over the years. Al Pacino, Dustin Hoffman, Sally Field, Madonna. I even worked on Goldie Hawn and Kurt Russell. Not for a movie. A Halloween party. Would you believe it? A Halloween party."

All the while Mark had been talking, he continued to prod and probe inside my mouth, shifting my face first in one direction, then in another. My neck and jaw had begun to ache.

"In this business, you not only have to be an artist but a plastic surgeon, a dentist, a cosmetician, an orthopedist. And now, even a computer wiz too.

"When I started out, it was just me. I've always worked on assignment. Except for the couple of years I worked for Columbia. And that was a mistake." He shrugged. "I never wanted any long-term commitment to any particular studio. Plus I didn't want to move to California." Mark moved around behind me and started kneading my jaw muscles. "I hate Los Angeles. All that smog.

"So I stayed here. Worked on Broadway and off-Broadway. Picked up a movie here and there. It was a nice life, and it was just me. Until *Dead Silence.*"

I couldn't tell Mark I remembered the film, so I tried to nod my acknowledgment.

"Be still," he snapped. "You'll mess everything up."

"After that movie," Mark continued his solo conversation, "the offers just poured in. So it was either expand, or give up all those millions.

"You wouldn't believe it, but I made over two million dollars last year alone. This is big business.

"I now have over twenty employees, most of whom are computer experts. They wouldn't know a tube of greasepaint if it bit them on the ass. It's really sad what they've missed. All the artistry, the imagination, the human contact." Mark pulled the plastic out of my mouth. I swallowed the bitter taste.

"Could I have some water?" I asked.

"Sure." He walked over to the sink and filled a paper cup with tap water, brought it back and handed it to me. I drank.

"Remember Cagney in *Man of a Thousand Faces*? Playing Lon Chaney, the movie star back in the twenties. *The Phantom of the Opera, Hunchback of Notre Dame.* Chaney did all his own makeup. Now there was a real magician. Nowadays, everything's computer graphics. The true makeup man is a thing of the past."

I moved my jaw, twisted my neck, trying to ease the dull pain in the bones and muscles.

"Can't complain, though. It's made me rich. I own the company outright, and the building too. Paid off the mortgage in only six years. That computer upstairs. It's not a PC, it's a mainframe. The network connects more than a dozen terminals throughout the building." Mark was working the plastic with his hands, shaping and forming. Then he took what looked like a scalpel and began scraping out a shape.

"You know how much that computer cost? Over five million dollars. That's the only thing I'm still paying off."

"Five million?" My first words in over half an hour sounded hollow and weak.

"Yep. Latest thing in technology, though. Only five of

them in the world right now. You can't do a movie these days without CEI."

"What's CEI?" I asked.

"Computer enhanced imagery. The things these computers can do, it goes beyond imagination. I can't begin to tell you."

Mark spent the next few minutes on what he was now calling my "mouth brace." He told me it would fit over the back of my bottom teeth, forcing my lower jaw to jut out slightly, eliminating the overbite I'd always had, and puffing out my cheeks. Mark also claimed it would not be visible when I talked or smiled, but it would create a completely different slant to my face. He said I could take it out at bedtime if I wanted, but he recommended leaving it in—it wouldn't be as painful that way, he assured. And, all the while he worked, he maintained his running monologue on computers.

"I hate to say it, 'cause it sounds like a cliché, but we ain't seen nothing yet. Twenty years ago the things today's computers can routinely do would have seemed almost unimaginable. So just think what twenty years from now will bring."

Mark spoke with considerable animation. I assumed this was a subject about which he felt very strongly.

"Take the movies, for instance. Right now, computers can meet most of the industry's special effects requirements. And you saw upstairs how still pictures can be created. The next step—and a logical one at that—is computer-generated motion pictures. Like *Jurassic Park*.

"And I'm not just talking pictures that move, like animation. You can already get computers to do that. I mean something like making the sequel to *Gone with the Wind* with the moving images of Clark Gable and Vivien Leigh. Computer images that are identical to the originals. Sound alike. Look alike. Gestures. Everything."

Mark walked over to the sink and turned on the tap.

"Just imagine. New Bette Davis films. Or John Wayne. Remember that movie Marilyn Monroe was making when she died—*Something's Got to Give?* Well, a computer will be able to finish it. And you'll never be able to tell the difference."

He held the plastic under the running water.

"Hell, we've already had computer-written novels. I don't know how good they are. But the point is—it's been done. And that's just the beginning. We're on the threshold of a total technological revolution. And we've been on that threshold for the past hundred years."

Mark ripped a paper towel from its roll, placed first the towel on the counter and then the plastic mold on the paper, then snapped on an arc light.

"It's like surfing, riding the crest of a wave. Well, we've just about found an endless wave. It's amazing—you can't keep up with the breakthroughs. Computers just five years old are now considered ancient. In this business, five years is an eternity."

He clicked off the light and picked up the mold. He brought it over to me, allowed me to inspect it, and then worked it into my mouth. As he fitted the hardened plastic into place, he said, "You'll experience a slight discomfort for a little while. But you'll soon get used to the brace, and pretty soon you won't even know you have it on."

I wasn't so sure of that. It was starting to hurt like hell.

Mark surveyed the effect, nodding in approval. He picked up a tube from the counter.

"What's that?" I asked.

"It's putty," he said. Mark squeezed a gob onto his hand, lifted the middle skin of my left ear, and smeared the putty behind it. Then he repeated the process on my right ear.

"Firm chin. Fatter cheeks. Protruding ears. Good." He handed me the mirror again.

"You'd be amazed," Mark added, "but ears can be a dead giveaway. But now, with your skin stretched taunt and with the putty in place, your ears don't look anything like they did before. The shape is definitely different."

He was right. I couldn't believe the change. The almost stranger I'd seen from my earlier look in the mirror had been replaced by a total stranger. I just shook my head.

"I can't believe it."

Mark smiled. My simple amazement seemed to please him more than any inadequate adjectives I could have offered. He handed me the tube of putty.

"This will wash right off every time you shower. So you'll need to reapply it yourself. There's enough here to last several days."

Mark pulled a white towel out of the cabinet and wiped his hands. Then, he turned his attention once again to me.

"Now, we'll fit you with some contact lenses. Add a chest protector that you can wear under your clothing—to add the appearance of a little more weight. And then I think we'll be done."

The contact lenses proved to be the most disconcerting. Mark showed me how to apply them to my eyes, and they went in easily enough. But the brown tint dimmed my vision. I felt I was wearing a dark pair of sunglasses—a very dark pair. After just a few minutes, my head began to hurt.

"Get up," Mark ordered. After three hours in the chair, it felt

OTHERWISE KNOWN AS MURDER

good to stand. I told Mark the contacts were giving me a headache.

"You'll get used to them," he said, without sympathy. He now draped a heavy vest around my shoulders, thicker at the bottom than at the top. It felt like it weighed ten pounds.

"Only five," said Mark, when I'd vocalized the thought.

"I've got some clothes for you upstairs in my apartment. And there's also a full-length mirror up there so that you can see the total picture. Then, after that, we'll unveil the new you to Lee."

Which is what we were now doing. She had just walked an entire circle around me.

"I can't believe it." At a loss for words, Lee had unknowingly parroted mine. "Mark, you are a genius. It's absolutely amazing.

"I can understand the hair and the eyes. But how did you change his whole face?"

Mark explained the mouth brace.

"Amazing," Lee said again. "I just realized it. He's shorter! Now how did you do that?"

"It's this vest," I said irritably. "It's so heavy, it pulls me down."

"It's not that heavy," Mark chided. "But Kyle's right. The weight does pull on his shoulders, which causes him to stoop just a bit. And that's what gives you the impression that he's shorter."

"And his voice—it sounds different."

"That's the mouth brace too," Mark acknowledged. "It forces the tongue to hit the teeth a little differently, and that results in a slightly altered pitch."

"It sounds like I'm talking in a tunnel," I complained.

Lee stepped back, assessing the result once more. "I knew you could do incredible things, Mark. But I wasn't prepared for this."

"Where's Bootsie?" I asked.

"She's over there asleep in the corner," Lee said somewhat distractedly, then, with more interest, "That's right. She hasn't seen you yet. Let's see how she reacts."

If Lee had hoped for consternation on Bootsie's part too, she was disappointed. After we'd called her awake, Bootsie came over to me, sniffed at my hands and trouser cuffs, got her head patted, then returned to her corner, curling up for more sleep. To dogs, maybe outward appearances aren't that important. It's a shame people aren't more that way.

"Okay, what's next?" Suddenly I felt impatient to be done with this.

"Now it's time to produce the physical evidence," said Mark. While Lee and I watched silently, Mark spent the next few minutes scurrying back and forth, moving furniture, setting up equipment, turning on lights. Once, I asked him if he needed any help, but he said no.

"It would take longer trying to explain to you what I wanted than just doing it myself," he said.

Finally, his industrious activity stopped, and he seemed pleased with the results. "Okay," he said, "now it's time for the stars."

Mark positioned Lee and me in front of a solid blue background, called to Bootsie, and somehow managed to get her to sit on her haunches at my feet. Then he went once again to his computer terminal.

"What I'm doing now," he told us, "is looking at you on the monitor. Kind of like closed-circuit TV. Lee, move a little to your left. Good. Kyle, see if you can get Bootsie to turn her head more toward the camera. That's fine. Now smile. Okay, that'll do it. Now come over here and watch the show."

Lee and I walked behind Mark, while Bootsie opted to remain where she was, sliding to a sleeping sprawl on the floor. How Mark had gotten her to pose so easily seemed to me the most truly stunning accomplishment of the day.

As Mark punched a variety of buttons on the keypad, I watched the picture on the screen shift, enlarge, sharpen. "What you're seeing now is basically what a photographer does in his darkroom. I'm adjusting the picture, cropping it, enhancing it. When I get it just right"—he hit another button—"I save it. Then I open a window and load in the boy's image that we completed this morning."

Suddenly Donny's face stared out from the screen, three times larger than Lee's and mine. A few more punches of the keys, and Donny not only retreated to scale, but he gained arms and legs and clothes. When Mark had made the adjustments that placed a standing and correctly proportioned Donny in front, and a little to the inside, of Lee, he held down two keys in combination and the computer hummed.

"Okay, I've just saved the image you see now on the screen," Mark said. He hit another key, then stood up. "Now I'll put a photographic cartridge in the special printer, and in about twenty minutes, we'll have a color picture to hold in our hands."

While we waited for the printer to do its job, Mark took a file folder from the drawer of the desk where he'd been sitting.

"After Lee called last night, I thought this might add a nice touch." He handed me a document. "It's Donny's birth certificate," Mark explained.

I read the information. Donald Ezra Malachi. "Ezra?" I asked. "Who in their right mind is named Ezra these days?"

"That's the whole point. It will give credibility to your story. You can say he was named for your grandfather."

"Neither of my grandfathers was named Ezra." I laughed.

"That doesn't matter. The whole thing's a fiction anyway. After Lee told me on the phone what it was the two of you were planning, the only information I asked for was the boy's first name, and your name of course. The rest all came either from personal knowledge"—he winked at Lee—"or from my own imagination."

I scanned the certificate. Father's Name—Kyle Malachi. Mother's Maiden Name—Lee Holland. Date of Birth—

"You've made him only sixteen years of age. I'm sure he was older than that," I protested.

"That doesn't matter either. He has to be underage to achieve your purpose."

I nodded my understanding.

Lee lifted the document from my hands. "Mark, it's beautiful. And you're absolutely right. It's the finishing touch. I just wish I'd thought of it."

The printer made a noise, and Mark went and retrieved the picture. "I think you'll be very pleased," he said as he presented it to Lee and me.

The photograph looked like a hundred, a thousand other similar shots. Mom, Dad, the kid, and the dog. The all-American family.

"The quality is superb," I commented. "It looks like a real picture."

"It is a real picture," said Mark.

"The Kyle Malachi family," said Lee. "I even believe it myself."

"But will anyone else believe it?" I asked.

Lee and I looked meaningfully at each other. We didn't have to say it; we both knew that was the only question that really mattered.

CHAPTER 12

*"This charming amateur sleuth is nothing
less than Nancy Drew for grown-ups."*
—*Stokes Moran,
on Mickey Friedman's* Magic Mirror

Lee and I flew into Houston the following day. How Lee had
managed to get plane tickets the day after Christmas seemed
to me a minor miracle in itself. When I asked, all she said was
"connections" and smiled. While hundreds of people scurried
to grab any available seats, we sailed through Kennedy, rode
in first-class comfort on an airline that showed how much it
loved to fly, and landed in Texas by mid-afternoon.

We had continued to refine the details of our plan last night.
Before we left Mark, he had printed out three more photographs—candid shots this time—revealing Donny in a variety of poses. One was just a head and shoulders shot—the
kind of picture you see all the time in high school yearbooks. Another showed him and Bootsie at play. The third, with hair a little longer, pictured Donny in a tuxedo, just the image of a
young boy decked out for his first prom. Then Mark had made
three sets of the lot, just in case we needed them. The things that
Mark could do with that computer defied logic. And reality.

It was past eight when we'd finally said good-bye to Mark,
and Bootsie. Lee and I had both agreed that there was no way

N E I L   M c G A U G H E Y

we could take the dog with us, but it was still hard leaving her
in the hands of a virtual stranger. Mark promised he would
take good care of her until our return (I really didn't doubt it,
armed as he was with all her favorite foods that I'd packed for
the occasion), and Lee assured me everything would be all
right for the few days we'd be gone, but still I worried. Leaving
Bootsie was always the most difficult part of any trip.

As I watched our two suitcases lobbed into the taxi's trunk,
I began to question the wisdom of our next move. At this
moment, it was still not too late to back out. Lee and I could
merely turn around, march back into the airport, and wait for
a return flight to New York. No harm done. Even the phone
call Lee had made to Houston two nights ago didn't commit
us to anything. If any questions were ever raised, I could
always pretend ignorance and pass it off as somebody's idea of
a bad joke.

But my chance to wimp out quickly passed. I held the taxi
door open for Lee, she gave the driver our destination, and the
two of us rode in mutual silence to the main downtown headquarters of the Houston Police Department.

* * *

Lee's plan—with some minor modifications offered by me—
was relatively simple. Since we both agreed that the murder
had been faked, that meant that Hedges and Donny were in it
together. Considering the complexity of the hoax, more people
were probably involved, but we knew those two had to be.
And, because of his age, Donny was the more accessible.
Pretending to be his parents gave us a legitimate entry into
New Orleans. We'd claim the boy had run away and that we

had come to find our son and take him back home. On the one-in-a-million chance that Donny really was dead—and, believe me, no one hoped more than I that we would find him very much alive—then we'd assume the role of grieving parents and take it from there. But we doubted that eventuality. Everything pointed in the opposite direction. Working out the details of the plan—including the calls to Mark Crews and the Houston Police Department—is how we had spent most of our Christmas Eve.

Now, as the taxi driver deposited us at police headquarters, we were poised to unleash our counterattack. Either our carefully crafted cover passed inspection, or we'd be sent packing. I hefted our bags and followed Lee into the building.

Three uniformed policemen stood behind a ten-foot-long counter just inside the doors. At least half a dozen people stood waiting for service while another three or four individuals occupied chairs in the middle of the room. I placed our luggage next to an empty seat, and remained there while Lee went to the counter to make our presence known. In a few minutes, I heard her ask for Lieutenant Dolan and receive mumbled instructions from a desk sergeant.

Lee motioned me to a doorway. I picked up the bags and followed her down a tiled corridor until we came to an opening that read "Missing Persons." We entered the area and found it deserted. I set the two bags down once again, this time with a measured degree of relief. After learning my lesson in New Orleans, I had insisted we each bring only one suitcase. Since I still got stuck carrying both, I hadn't really accomplished my objective. But it was at least a start in the right direction.

Carting our luggage to police headquarters had been one of

Lee's little details that she felt gave added credibility to our story. Distraught parents would surely go straightaway to the police, she'd asserted, and not bother to check into a hotel first. I didn't doubt her logic, but then she didn't have to carry the damn things.

"Yes?" A man had emerged from a doorway on the right side of the room. Short and leaning to fat, he took quick jerking steps toward us. As he approached, he patted the few wisps of hair on his head in what must have been a habitual manner to cover his baldness.

"Are you Lieutenant Dolan?" asked Lee. When he nodded, Lee identified herself as Mrs. Kyle Malachi. "I spoke with you two nights ago from Connecticut."

"Yes ma'am."

"Have you found our son?" Lee didn't waste any time getting to the point.

"Well, ma'am"—Lieutenant Dolan had a pronounced Texas drawl— "as I told you on the phone, we'll have to have more to go on. You were pretty nonspecific the other evening." I had heard her side of the conversation; incoherent would have been a more apt description.

"I'm sorry if I didn't make myself clear. But hopefully you understand. My husband and I just want to find our son." I heard Lee muffle a sob and thought what a hell of an actress.

"Yes ma'am, I know." Had Dolan's tone become more sympathetic? "You and your husband just come on back here and we'll get all the necessary papers filled out."

I had to give it to Lee, so far so good. She and I followed the lieutenant to a desk against the back wall. There were only two chairs—one for him and one for her. Dolan didn't make an effort to locate another chair, so I stood while Lee answered the lieutenant's questions.

We'd selected Houston for two reasons. First, we needed a major metropolitan area geographically close to New Orleans. We figured the case would get less attention from a big-city police force, what with all the other foibles of mankind they daily encountered. Easier to get lost in the shuffle, so to speak. And we had to get the boy's disappearance on the record somewhere. Houston was as good a place as any.

And second, Lee had a friend who was headmaster at Dexter Military Academy in Lakehurst, on the outskirts of Houston. That gave us a working familiarity with the place, in case we needed specifics. Painting Donny as a runaway from a military school was not only in keeping with the regimented behavior I'd observed in the boy, but it provided a reasonable and logical explanation to his disappearance—he had run because he hated the school. Simple as that. Lee had not felt it necessary to enlist the cooperation of the headmaster ("Let's hope they don't check," she had argued, "but even if they do, school's out for the holidays. By the time they get around to backtracking our story, maybe this will all be over.").

The lieutenant had finished with all the vital statistics, and now he was delving into riskier territory.

"How long has the boy been missing?"

"We don't really know." Lee had the answer ready. "We haven't heard from him since before Thanksgiving when he sent us a postcard saying he would be spending the holiday with a friend he'd met at school. We had no reason to believe otherwise."

"Okay." Dolan jotted that information down. "Then when was the last time you actually saw your son?" asked Dolan.

"September."

"Yeah," I interjected, ready with the spin we'd agreed would make the police dismiss our case without expending too much effort on our behalf. "That's when we shipped him off to Dexter. For his own good."

"Now, Kyle."

"You know it's the truth, Lee." I appealed to the lieutenant. "What would you do if a son of yours suddenly decided he was homosexual?" The way I strung out the syllables of the word—making it sound as loathsome as I could—would leave no doubt in Lieutenant Dolan's mind on where I stood on the subject. "And then announced it openly to you? Like he was proud of it or something." I shot Lee a disgusted look. "Wouldn't you try to make a man—"

Lee interrupted, with noticeable irritation. "Kyle, the lieutenant doesn't want to hear all this. It has absolutely no bearing on Donny's disappearance."

"I wouldn't be too sure of that, Mrs. Malachi," said Dolan. "I've seen kids run for all sorts of reasons. Sex is as good as any of 'em." He abruptly stood. "Let me see what I can do."

The scene had worked, just as we'd hoped, just as we'd rehearsed. Anyone could see the immediate and striking change in Dolan's attitude. No longer the solicitous policeman, he had suddenly turned into an officious cop. This man demonstrated a typical macho rejection of anything that did not conform to his rigid notion of normalcy, to his narrow concept of right and wrong. Lee and I had counted on a similar stereotypical reaction, but never in our wildest imaginations had we anticipated so effective a result. It was all I could do to keep from sweeping Lee up in my arms in triumph.

Lee rose from her chair as well, clutching her handbag in worry. "How long will it take, do you think? Will you be able to find our son?" Her voice trembled, with fear, with concern. She'd even convinced me of her mother's anxiety, and I knew better. Imagine the effect her performance was having on Dolan.

"It's hard to say, Mrs. Malachi. I wouldn't give up hope, but your son's probably been gone for several weeks now. It's not going to be easy to pick up his trail." He walked around the desk and herded us toward the door. "Thousands of kids run away from home every year. Most of them stay lost." Seeing the discouraged look on Lee's face, he added softly but firmly, "But we'll do everything we can."

"Thank you, Lieutenant," Lee said. The three of us now stood in the hallway. "When should we check back with you?"

Dolan hesitated. "What with the holidays and all, and being understaffed here, I'd say sometime after the first of the year." Never is what he really meant. "Will you be staying in Houston?"

"No, I don't think so." Lee turned away from the lieutenant, ready to head back down the corridor. "I think we'll try New Orleans."

"That's not a bad idea," said Dolan. "That city has a large homosexual community." I heard first the disgust, then the relief as he added, "Not like Houston." Whether that assertion was true or not, it was clear Dolan willingly chose to believe it.

"Thank you, Lieutenant Dolan," Lee said, ready to depart. "You've been awfully kind." Then, as if she'd suddenly remembered, she exclaimed, "I almost forgot. I have a picture of Donny. Won't that help?" Lee searched frantically through her purse, pulled out one of the snapshots, and thrust it at the lieutenant.

Caught off-guard, Dolan said somewhat lamely, "You gave me the boy's description." Then, seeming to think better of his response, or perhaps seeing the nakedly hopeful look on Lee's face, Dolan added, "Sure." He accepted the photo without even glancing at it. "I'll add this to the file. This will help a lot."

I shook his hand, then picked up the two suitcases, and Lee and I took our good-byes from the ever-helpful Lieutenant Dolan, and the Houston Police Department.

* * *

"That was beautiful." Lee held her words until we were outside, and standing on the building's steps. She was laughing. "It went even better than I'd expected."

"Well, you're responsible," I declared. "You're the one who did it. You had him eating right out of your hand. Now, tell me Ms. Streep, just where did you learn to act like that?"

Lee clowned. "When you're an agent, you learn to fake it."

"Oh really," I kidded back. "Are you saying you have to fake it a lot?"

"Exactly. When you have clients who aren't quite as good as they think they are, you have to massage their egos a little, that's all."

"Any clients I know?" I joked.

"Not you, if that's what you're asking." The laugh lines eased just a fraction from around her eyes. "I never had to fake it with you."

Avoiding any further discussion of that topic, I dropped the luggage on the pavement. "These bags are heavy," I commented. "We should have called a taxi from inside."

CHAPTER 13

"This novel, through its gentle and compas-
sionate persuasion, reminds us that we all
have debts—many that we aren't even aware
we owe—that sooner or later must be paid."
　　　　　　　　　　　—*Stokes Moran,*
　　　　　　　　　on Nancy Pickard's I.O.U.

Returning to New Orleans was a calculated gamble. It would
be the first real test of the effectiveness of my disguise. Nobody
in Houston had ever seen me before. But I'd been in New
Orleans only five days earlier. I had met people, talked to
them, been seen by them, interacted with them, been conned
by them. And I had to keep reminding myself—that had been
Stokes Moran. So would anyone recognize the physically
altered Kyle Malachi? That was the question uppermost on my
mind the following day as Lee and I approached the Crescent
City from the west on Interstate 10.

After our success with the Houston police, Lee and I had
checked into a motel on the eastern side of the Texas city. We'd
had a tough couple of days, and we needed the rest. Tired of
flying, I'd suggested we rent a car and drive the four hundred
or so miles to New Orleans. Plus, I had argued, it would give
us the opportunity to carefully map out our next few moves.
We'd been traveling so fast I told Lee I had the feeling events

had started to control us, instead of the other way around. She agreed with all my points without objection.

At eight o'clock that morning, after an early but leisurely breakfast and a brisk taxi ride to Avis, I had climbed behind the wheel of a navy blue Lincoln Mark V, Lee had taken up her navigator's post in the seat next to me, and we had set off for New Orleans. And the unknown and unpredictable next leg of our adventure.

* * *

Twilight had come to the flat Louisiana bayou country. I snapped on the car's headlights, and Lee stirred from her sleep.

"What time is it?" she asked.

"It's almost five," I answered. "You've been sacked out for almost three hours." Ever since we'd stopped for lunch, at which time I'd also had the tank filled and the car serviced.

"How much farther?" She sounded a little bit cranky. Naps will do that to you.

"I figure another half hour or so."

"It's almost dark." She stretched out her legs and raised her arms over her head, her fingertips brushing against the car's ceiling.

"Yes, isn't it." I avoided the obvious "How observant of you!" or "What did you expect?" but she still thought my remark sarcastic.

"Testy, aren't we?"

"I didn't think so."

"Well, I did." Lee didn't respond with her normal cheerfulness, so I let the conversation lapse. After a few minutes, she picked it up again.

"Are you ready?" I knew what she meant, but I couldn't resist a "Ready for what?"

She groaned. "Talking to you is impossible," she said, but this time I could hear an amused affection in her voice.

"It's better than Bootsie," I kidded.

"Don't be so sure. But since Bootsie's not here, I guess you'll have to do."

"Thank you."

"Don't thank me. Thank Bootsie." This time we both laughed.

"Tell me," Lee said, after we'd driven another mile in silence, "seriously this time, are you ready?"

"I guess so. I know one thing—I want to find out." Find out if it had been a hoax, find out if the boy was alive, find out if I could get my revenge, find out (as Lee was asking) if I could go through with the whole thing.

"Yes, I'm ready," I asserted, with growing authority, after just the briefest of pauses.

"Good," said Lee. "So am I."

* * *

That morning we'd decided we wouldn't go to the police first, as we had in Houston. So, with Lee directing, I took the St. Charles exit off the interstate and headed for the Hilton. We had discussed staying at the Queen Royale but had agreed that might be pushing our luck too far. At least for the time being.

I pulled the car into the hotel's parking garage and collected our luggage from the trunk. Lee walked on ahead and had the elevator waiting by the time I caught up with her.

The Hilton—a square, squat building—sits on Poydras,

right off Canal, just on the edge of the French Quarter. Close
enough, without being too close.

Lee approached the registration desk and rang for the clerk
while I gratefully let the bags sag to the floor. Hopefully, this
would be the last time I'd have to carry these burdensome
things without someone else's assistance.

"I'm Mrs. Kyle Malachi," I heard Lee say. "I phoned in
reservations this morning."

"Yes ma'am. Let me check." The man keyed the computer.
After a minute, he said, "I have you in Room 612. Front." He
hit the bell.

Suddenly my heart was in my throat. The scene had been
so reminiscent of my earlier arrival at another New Orleans
hotel that for half a heartbeat I thought I'd see Donny answer
the summons. But it was an older, grayer, less energetic, noth-
ing-at-all-like-Donny bellman who responded.

He guided us to our room, accepted a five-dollar tip with no
acknowledgment whatsoever, and departed without ever once
having said a single word to us. Lee flopped down on one of
the double beds.

"Well, here we are. Downtown Big Easy. What do you want
to do now?"

"Eat. Drink."

"Be merry," she added.

We both left the rest unsaid.

* * *

Our encounter with the New Orleans police the following
morning did not go that much differently from the way it
had with Houston's finest. But there was one major varia-

tion—the homophobia was not as pronounced. In fact, it was the exact opposite.

After I ended my sanctimonious speech about making a man out of the boy, Sergeant Colbert showed no sudden about-face. In addition, he chastised me for not being more open to my son's sexual preference.

"A sixteen-year-old boy is likely to be confused about his sexual nature," said the sergeant. "What you need to do is offer him the support and guidance he needs to get him through this difficult time."

Lee and I smiled, and almost gave away our cover. Colbert looked at us quizzically.

"Did I say something funny?"

"Oh no." Lee quickly covered our lapse. "It's just I've said basically the same thing for the past six months."

Sergeant Colbert nodded. This was a man I was finding it hard not to like. For the first time, I felt some guilt in the lie we were perpetrating. I wondered if Lee felt the same thing.

Colbert was younger than his counterpart in Houston. Maybe it was his age that made him more accepting of human nature. But his youth and attitude were not his only departures from Dolan.

Tall and thin, Colbert had a Cajun look about him—black hair, black eyes, swarthy complexion. He was clean-shaven and, from the mass of hair on his head, would never have to worry about baldness. He also had a toothy grin that came easily, even when discussing something as serious as the disappearance of a child or the lifestyle choice the boy had made. And he was smarter than the Houston cop too.

I decided that I did indeed like Colbert, and that made me

wary. We couldn't afford to make any mistake where he was concerned. I felt sure he'd arrest us for filing a false report. He had that no-nonsense air about him, and an obvious and admirable dedication to his job. I'm sure he made a good cop. Honest, honorable, he probably came from a couple of generations of policemen.

"Wouldn't you say so, dear?" Lee's question pulled me back from my speculations on Colbert's character. I had no idea what had been said, but Lee saw my confusion and repeated, "That Donny's likely to come home on his own?"

"Possibly. After he gets this foolishness out of his system." I still had to maintain my stance as the unaccepting father. Colbert frowned.

"I think you're being naive here, Mr. Malachi. Most of the young boys who come to New Orleans have pretty much come to a decision. It's not a question of getting anything out of their systems. It's more that they've made a break with their pasts. Most don't ever go home again."

"Well, that's not Donny," said Lee. "I'm sure if we could just talk to him, and if Kyle could show just a bit more understanding, he'd come home with no problem."

"I'm afraid you don't understand runaways, Mrs. Malachi," said Colbert, with a trace of sadness and regret. "They find that life on their own is tough, that it's nothing like they were used to. Mostly, it's worse. Much worse." He picked up the family portrait Lee had remembered to proffer much earlier in this interview. "Looking at this photo, I'd say your boy has probably learned quite a few lessons since he disappeared. And I'd say they haven't been easy to take."

"What do you mean?" Lee asked.

"I don't want to paint too grim a picture," he said, "but your son is good-looking. Very good-looking. I don't have to tell you that. And, believe me, there are bad people who will exploit those looks, exploit him."

"Are you saying he's turned into a whore?" I almost shouted.

Lee audibly gasped at my graphic depiction. Colbert responded. "Not willingly, I'm sure, Mr. Malachi. But, as I said, life for a kid on the run is tough. It's not easy making money, getting food, keeping warm, or finding a place to stay. People will do almost anything just to meet their basic needs. Who's to say that whatever they turn to in such circumstances is wrong?"

"I do. No son of mine is going to sell his body. I'd rather have him dead." I hated having to come across as such a jerk to this sympathetic and caring man.

Lee started to sob, and Colbert glared angrily at me. "If I do manage to find your son for you, Mr. Malachi, I can promise you this. Before I turn him back over to you, your attitude will have to change. Whatever he's done to survive, accept it. Accept him."

I nodded. It was time to ease up on the holier-than-thou routine. Colbert's last words indicated that demonstrating too rigid a father image could potentially derail our entire plan.

"Sergeant, my husband's just as worried as I am," Lee said, helping pull me back from the brink. "He just shows it with anger instead of with tears."

"I understand your concern, Mrs. Malachi, and I'll do everything I can to find your boy. And I'll check with Houston PD to see if they've come up with anything. But don't get your hopes up. As I said, kids determined to get lost usually do."

"But if he's in New Orleans . . ." Lee left her question unasked.

"If he's in New Orleans, there's a good chance we'll locate him."

"That's all we ask."

"What happens after that," Colbert added, looking me directly in the eyes, "is all up to you."

* * *

Shortly before noon, after letting Sergeant Colbert know how we could be reached if he came up with anything, Lee and I left the midtown police station. It had started to rain, and we scampered to our car in the cold steady drizzle.

"Ready for lunch?" I asked.

"Yes," Lee answered absently.

I unlocked the passenger door of the Lincoln, touched the electronic button to unlock my side as well, and held the door open for Lee. She slipped in, and I closed the door behind her, then walked around and got behind the wheel. With seat belts in place, I turned to her and asked, "Where to?"

"I don't care." Lee stared straight ahead, her voice a monotone, her desolate mood an appropriate match for the weather.

"I know how you feel," I said, believing I could read Lee's thoughts. "I hated deceiving such a good man too."

"It all seemed like such a lark before, especially with that asshole in Houston. It was all going to be such fun. Just us versus them. The good guys take on the bad guys. The fuzz. The heat. Not real people at all. Just characters in a play. Our play. But now. . . ." Her voice trailed off.

"I know." I put the car in gear and eased out of the parking lot, heading in the general direction of our hotel. "Now we can see the human cost, the number of man-hours the police will devote to searching for Donny, the wasted concern of a dedicated officer."

"Exactly," Lee agreed. "It's not just a game anymore."

"No it's not," I concurred. "Let's just hope they find him fast."

We lunched at an Italian restaurant on Canal. The food was passable, but within a mile from where we now spooned and forked were many of the world's finest and most famous restaurants. I said as much to Lee.

"Kyle, we agreed to avoid the French Quarter until the police find the boy," Lee responded. "Unless several days go by and they come up empty. Then we'll try our luck."

"Okay then, what do we do in the meantime?"

"We wait."

Lee and I finished our meal in virtual silence, neither one of us feeling much like talking, or eating for that matter. When the waitress cleared our plates, she commented on our mutual lack of appetite.

"Not hungry, I guess," I said.

"Not the food, I hope." The waitress showed genuine concern.

"No, no, not at all," I assured her, even if it was a bit of a lie.

After the waitress left, Lee and I put on our coats and headed back out into the rainy afternoon. I turned up my coat collar for protection against the icy wind. For a while, we both stood unmoving under the restaurant's overhanging canopy.

"Now where?" I finally asked.

"I don't know," said Lee. "And I don't particularly care.

Let's just get in the car and drive." Which is what we did, and at a relatively leisurely pace.

Neither Lee nor I were strangers to this city, my familiarity with New Orleans naturally more recent than hers, so we had a fairly accurate working knowledge of the general lay of the land. With the rain pelting the windshield, it somehow seemed appropriate to head for more water.

The Lake Pontchartrain Causeway is an engineering marvel. Purportedly the world's longest open-water bridge, it stretches flat and straight across the lake's surface for more than twenty-five miles. Only the requisite shipping channels—forming massive camel's humps in the dual span of concrete—break its straight gray lines. And the color of the day was definitely gray. Gray causeway. Gray water. Gray sky. Gray spirits.

By the time we'd reached the far shore, I was ready to abandon our excursion. Lee voiced no objection as I maneuvered the Lincoln through a highway crossover and headed back to New Orleans. The return trip was just as bleak. Forty minutes later, as I braked to a stop inside the Hilton's parking garage, I realized that neither of us had spoken since we'd left the restaurant, and we didn't interrupt the silence until we stepped off the elevator into the hotel lobby.

"Better check for messages," I suggested.

Lee nodded and walked over to the front desk. I watched her quiz the clerk, then she trudged slowly back in my direction.

"Anything?" I asked, when she had rejoined me.

"Nothing we weren't expecting," she said. "Donny's been found."

CHAPTER 14

"The boy was heroic and brave and coura-
geous. But most of all he was human. And
that, above all else, is what makes him
unforgettable."

—*Stokes Moran,*
on Sue Grafton's "C" Is for Corpse

"I keep telling you—they're not my parents!"

For the third or fourth time since Lee and I had arrived at police headquarters, Donny vehemently shouted his protest.

"I don't know him! I don't know her!" He pointed at each of us in turn, then furiously grabbed the photograph off the desk. "And I sure as hell don't know this dog!"

"That is you in the picture, isn't it?" Sergeant Colbert asked.

"It can't be!" he screamed. "It has to be some kind of trick!" Donny plopped down in a chair and glared angrily at Lee and me.

Sergeant Colbert spoke. "Mr. and Mrs. Malachi, I don't know what to say. Nothing like this has ever happened before, not in my experience at least."

"This is our son," Lee assured the sergeant, then she turned toward the boy. "Donny, I don't know why you keep denying it."

The boy leaped from his chair. "Why are you doing this?" Donny implored, moving to within a foot of her.

"Honey"—Lee reached out to touch him, but the boy shied back—"we love you. We want you to come back home."

"Hell!" Donny stormed toward Colbert. "You're not buying this bullshit are you?"

"Truthfully, I don't know what to buy," said Colbert, employing Donny's expression.

"Look," Donny entreated, "either these people are loonies or they're perverts, I don't know which. But whatever they are, they're not my parents! My parents are dead!"

"Oh, Donny," Lee moaned.

Colbert pushed back his chair and stood behind his desk. "Mr. and Mrs. Malachi, I'll level with you. My gut tells me something's not right. I've had kids in here who've yelled bloody murder at their parents, who've threatened and pleaded and cried. I've had kids to throw up, kids to shake in fear of their lives, and kids to try and break out. But I've never—ever—had a kid to say that the people claiming to be his parents weren't really his parents at all. Not till now."

"Sergeant—" Lee began.

"Wait, let me finish. There's something else. In this business, we don't have a very high success rate. Most of the time we aren't able to locate the missing kids, and we have to disappoint a lot of parents. But on those lucky occasions when we do manage to track a kid down, it usually takes days, sometimes even weeks or months. Today, when I find your son at the second place I look, well, I don't know. It was just too easy, and that bothers me." He walked in front of his desk, leaned back against it, and folded his arms across his chest. "It bothers me a lot."

Donny turned toward Colbert. "See, what did I tell you!"

"Hold on, son," the sergeant said. "I don't buy your story completely either. After I got an ID on you at the hotel, and while I was waiting for you to get back to the lobby, I had a chance to look at your personnel records."

Hotel? Had Colbert found Donny at the Queen Royale? Maybe the boy had just taken a couple of days off after all, as I had suggested to Lee back on Christmas Eve. But why would he do so without telling anyone? And did they just take him back on the job with no questions asked? Or had he gone to work at some other hotel? I decided it would be best not to ask, but something definitely seemed fishy.

"There's something fishy there." Colbert's choice of words startled me. At first I thought he was reading my mind, then I realized he was still referring to Donny's personnel records. "I think you falsified your application."

Donny stared down at the floor. Sergeant Colbert continued, "After I brought you back here, I ran a check on the Social Security number you had given the hotel. It belongs to a . . ." The sergeant picked up a piece of paper from his desk and read from it. ". . . a Mavis Conroy in Little Rock, Arkansas. How do you explain that?" The sergeant placed the sheet of paper once again on the desktop. Donny looked more sullen than ever, and he plopped back down in the chair he had recently vacated.

Sergeant Colbert continued, "Now I'm not saying either that they are your parents or that they're not your parents." Donny's body sagged even deeper into the cushions of the chair. "I'm only saying I have . . . questions." He left the word hanging ominously, a challenge to Lee and me.

"Sergeant, I don't know anything about policework," Lee

answered. "And I can't explain why Donny's acting the way he is. All I know is I'm his mother, and he's my son. And I want him back." Chalk up another Oscar-winning performance for Ms. Lee Holland. Er, Mrs. Kyle Malachi.

"Oh," Lee added. "I forgot to give you this." She searched through her purse and came out with a folded document. "It's Donny's birth certificate."

The sergeant took the paper from Lee's outstretched hand, looked it over, and shook his head. Then, he walked over to Donny.

"Son," Colbert handed him the document, "how do you explain this?"

Donny examined the paper, and a look of momentary panic crossed his face. Then, he rebounded.

"Ezra? My name's not Ezra. This is crazy."

"Ezra was his great-grandfather's name," Lee volunteered. "Donny's always hated it."

"Son, I think you're outnumbered," Colbert admitted. "They've got the evidence. The pictures. The birth certificate. That's more than most parents come with." The sergeant turned and spoke directly to Lee and me. "Usually people are too distraught to remember to bring such things. I want to thank you for being so helpful." I could recognize sarcasm, even when it wasn't mine.

Donny still had some fight left in him. "I don't care what they've got, and I don't know how they got it. They're not my parents!"

Colbert offered Donny one last chance. "Son, do you have anything to disprove their claim? Any identification? Anything at all?"

You could see the defeat show on Donny's face. Slowly he shook his head.

"Then I have no choice. As far as I can tell, these people are who they say they are—your parents—and, since I have no reason to hold you, I'm going to release you into their custody." He then turned a cold eye toward me, and added, "Hopefully, you'll be able to work all this out among yourselves."

* * *

"At least we definitely know you're not a murderer," said Lee, once we were back in our hotel room.

"Yeah, that's a relief," I said. Even though I had never truly believed I could possibly have killed another human being, my actions had not distinguished me as a man of character or compassion. I had taken the expedient course, running away instead of dealing with the situation. If I had stayed in that hotel room, if I had checked the body, if I had cared at all about the human being in that bed—all the terror I had felt, all the guilt I had experienced, all the rules I had broken—all that could easily have been prevented.

Donny, strangely docile since Sergeant Colbert had turned him over to us, had retreated into the bathroom as soon as we'd walked in the door. I had stayed close to him ever since the police station, just in case he suddenly decided to bolt. But he never once made the least move to run.

"That's a relief," I said, shucking my jacket and tie, dropping both onto the top of the writing table. "I don't have to tell you I was sweating bullets there for a while."

"Well, you're in the clear now."

"Yeah, but what about the boy? What do we do with him?"

"Well, your disguise must be pretty good. He still hasn't recognized you." That didn't surprise me; several times over the past few days when I'd looked in a mirror, I hadn't recognized myself, either.

"Well, he might not know who we are, but he definitely knows we're not his parents."

"That's for sure. I thought there for a minute the sergeant was more inclined to believe him than us."

"I think it was for more than a minute," I said. "The sergeant's no fool. And I'm sure he's seen all kinds of scams in his time. But that birth certificate really did the trick."

"Mark came through on that one." Lee opened her purse and took out the fake document, appraising it once again. "It really does look authentic," she said. "And it took the wind right out of Donny's sails."

"Yeah, when the boy saw that, he just kind of withered up and died."

"But even with that, Colbert didn't seem a hundred percent convinced we were Donny's parents." Lee frowned. "I'm sure he still has his doubts. But he probably can't figure out what our angle could be if we're not who we say we are."

"What do you mean?"

"For one thing, who but the kid's parents would go to this much trouble to get him back? And if we're not his parents, why go to the police?" Lee sat down on the edge of the bed. "Anybody outside the law—mobsters, drug dealers, white slavers—would just grab the kid. They wouldn't fool with the police—they wouldn't take the chance."

"White slavers? You have a vivid imagination, Lee."

"It's not that farfetched, Kyle. Donny's a good-looking kid, and I'm sure there are pornographers or pedophiles out there who would pay handsomely to have him in their clutches."

"But we're not any of those things. We're the all-American family, remember?" I walked over to where Lee sat and put my arm around her. "That was the one thing the sergeant couldn't ignore."

Lee smiled. "You're right; he couldn't dismiss that. But I think he still has his doubts."

"Well, even if he's not quite convinced of our story, we'll be long gone before he'll be able to do anything about it."

"I wouldn't be too sure about that, Kyle. I think we need to get this over with fast and get back home. That sergeant doesn't strike me as someone to mess around with."

"Well, if the boy can lead us to Severe, we won't have to waste any more concern on the sergeant." I stood up. "What's that kid doing in there all this time anyway?"

Lee kicked off her shoes, pulled a pillow out from under the bedspread, fluffed it, folded it, then leaned back against it. "He's probably trying to figure out what's going on. After all, he must be pretty confused right about now."

I walked toward the bathroom door. "I know he can't escape," I whispered back to Lee. "There's no window in there." Suddenly I had another thought. "Do you think he's trying to kill himself?"

"I wouldn't think so." Abruptly Lee bolted upright, alarm in her voice. "Kyle, your razor's in there. You don't suppose—"

I stood at the bathroom door, arm raised to pound, when it opened. Donny casually sauntered into the room, totally nude.

* * *

It took Lee and me a moment to shift away from our anxiety over Donny's potential suicide and confront the reality of a naked boy standing in our midst. I was the first to react.

"What the hell! Put on some clothes."

"I thought this was what you wanted." Donny smirked. "A little three-way?"

Lee was standing now as well, her mouth open in shock. I jerked the comforter off the bed nearest me and wrapped it around the boy's shoulders.

"Hey, what's the idea?" protested Donny. Then, clearly confused, he added, "I don't understand."

"You've got us wrong, kid," I said. "That's not what we want."

"It's what all adults want," Donny responded belligerently. "I learned that a long time ago."

"How old are you, boy?" I asked.

"You should know," Donny said smugly, "you're my parents."

"Cut the crap, kid." Lee had regained her composure. "We all know the score. Now answer the man. How old are you?"

Donny, not yet willing to play it straight, responded, "The birth certificate you have says I'm sixteen."

I grabbed his shoulder, the comforter slipped, and he reached to grab it before it fell to the floor. "How old, boy?"

Donny grudgingly answered, as if it were something of which he was ashamed. "I'm twenty-two—all right. Are you satisfied now?" I was more relieved than satisfied, but I didn't tell him that.

"But I can pass for fifteen," Donny continued. "Guys will pay big bucks for what they think is chicken."

"Chicken?" I asked.

"Yeah, you know. Young meat, fresh flesh, underage punk. Chicken."

I tried not to let the revulsion show in my face. It wasn't directed at Donny, but more at a society that turns blind eyes to such activities. Then Donny appended, with somewhat a defensive quiver to his voice, "Hey man, it's a living."

I didn't want to pursue this topic of conversation. "Go put your clothes on." I pushed him toward the bathroom. "And be quick about it," I added.

* * *

This time Donny was in and out of the bathroom in less than two minutes. He walked back into the bedroom still stuffing his shirttail into the top of his Levi's.

"That's better," I said.

Even though I now knew his real age, I continued to think of Donny as a boy. He certainly looked and acted childlike. Questions assaulted my brain. What kind of world does this boy inhabit? I wondered dejectedly. And what kind of people make such a world possible?

"Now let's cut this bullshit," I said, "and get down to business."

"Fine with me," said Donny, with a returning reassurance to his words. "Just what business do you have in mind?"

Lee and I had discussed this moment, prepared for it, debated it. Now that it had arrived, I wasn't sure how to proceed.

"Do you recognize me?" I finally asked.

"Yeah, man, you're my daddy."

Donny's reassurance had turned into sarcasm. I heard Lee mutter, "Like father, like son." I stifled the impulse to laugh, and repeated, "Do you recognize me?"

He shifted from foot to foot. "Naw, man." Donny met my eyes for the first time, then turned serious. "No sir, I don't recognize you. Should I?"

The boy was a contradiction in character, in emotion. One minute he could be swaggering and sexual, the next intense and thoughtful. Even his language changed to fit his mood. A chameleon, I thought. He projects whatever image he feels fits the situation. How had he learned the technique? Had he developed it as a survival mechanism? Or was Donny just a born actor?

"Yes you should," I said. "Only I few days ago I murdered you."

I had expected a number of responses—denial, outrage, panic—but not laughter. Donny hooted, he hollered, he roared.

"Oh, man," he said, when the laughing spasm had passed, "I never thought I'd see you again. And what did you do to yourself?" He walked a circle around me. "It's fucking unbelievable."

"Watch your language, young man." Lee spoke for the first time in some minutes.

"Sorry, ma'am." No question, Donny had a streak of courtesy in him. "It's just so radical. I never would have recognized you, man. You could have gone on jerking my chain forever."

"That wasn't the idea." Lee took over the conversation, explaining briefly how we had altered my appearance, and then for what purpose. "Now we need your help," she appealed to Donny.

"What can I do?"

"First, you can start by telling us everything you know, everything you did."

"May I sit down?" The boy's on-again off-again politeness seemed to be an instinctual part of his personality. Was it possible that his rougher, ruder traits were the false cover—the affected behavior—and this the real Donny?

He flopped down in one of the side chairs, and Lee and I perched on the side of the bed nearest him.

"Now what is it you want to know?"

"Why don't you just start talking?" Lee prompted.

"Well," he stretched back in the chair, "it was all Matty's idea." Donny looked at Lee. "Matthew Hedges." Then he glanced at me. "He knows who I mean."

Lee nodded. "Go on."

"The night you arrived, Matty told me somebody was coming in from outta town he wanted to burn real bad."

"Burn?" I asked.

"You know, fake out. Gas."

"Oh, you mean trick."

"No, man, where I come from, trick means something entirely different." The boy's smile, the first in my presence, changed the demeanor of the moment. All hostility disappeared, all suspicion and uncertainty. It was an open, winning, friendly smile. And it was contagious.

"You were saying Matty wanted to burn Kyle," Lee encouraged.

"That's right," continued Donny. "He wanted to burn him real bad."

"Did he say why?"

Donny shook his head. "What he told me was that the man was an old college friend of his who had gotten him good once with a practical joke and that he wanted to get even. But I didn't buy it." He shifted his gaze to me. "Not after I saw you."

"Why was that?" I asked.

"It was clear you two were strangers, that you didn't know Matty at all."

"Did you question Matty about it?" asked Lee.

"No ma'am. I was getting a Benji, so I didn't care."

"A Benji?" I asked.

"Yessir, a hundred dollars. A Benji."

In books and movies, it's a C-note, but Benji was a new one on me. I could figure out the reason easily enough, though— short for Benjamin Franklin, whose face adorned the hundred-dollar bill. I decided to remember the slang for possible use in my novel. If I ever get back to it, that is.

"Anyway, what did I care what Matty's reason was? I was getting paid. He told me what to do, and I did it. It was as simple as that."

"Just what was it you did?" Lee asked.

Donny appeared to be tiring of the interrogation. "He told me Mr. Moran—hey, I just realized, you changed your name too—he told me Mr. Moran might be asking some questions and if he did to steer him to Murder on the Levee and to Fido's. He said to make sure he got those two names."

"Did he say why?"

"No ma'am. Matty didn't tell me much. But he and Manny—Manny's the owner of Murder on the Levee—are close. You know, buddy-buddy. So I thought he had probably set up something with him."

"And Fido's?" I asked.

"I never heard of Fido's. Far as I know, Matty made it up."

I was confused. "But you gave me the directions. And I went to Fido's. I was there."

"I just said what Matty told me to say. All I had to do was to get you to a general location—on Bourbon Street somewhere around the Tail of the Cock restaurant—and Matty would take it from there."

"But you took me back to the hotel. That was you, wasn't it?"

"Yeah, it was me." Donny leaned forward in the chair, propping his head on his arms. "Matty told me to meet him there on the street at 2 A.M. I waited for about half an hour and when I finally saw him, he was just about carrying you."

"Then the two of you managed to get Kyle back to his hotel room."

"That's right. I had the key, and I let Matty and Mr. Moran—Mr. Malachi—into the room."

"Then what?" Lee asked.

Donny looked to me. "You were really out of it, man. I thought you were drunk—"

"Drugged," I amended.

"Whatever."

"Then what?" Lee persisted.

Donny shifted again in his seat. "Look, lady, I don't know how to say this, so—Matty wanted to find out if Mr. Moran was, well, you know . . . gay." Donny had trouble voicing the word.

"Whatever for?" I demanded.

"I don't know. Maybe he had the hots for you himself. I just don't know."

N E I L   M c G A U G H E Y

"So you—" Lee prompted.

"So I went in the bathroom, worked myself up, and came out on the make." Donny spat out the admission.

"Look, I'm not happy with what I did, man. But bread is bread. And this was easier than most."

Then he turned to Lee. "Nothing happened, ma'am. I don't know if your husband was too juiced up or if he just wasn't interested. But nothing happened. Except he passed out cold."

Lee took over the story. "And while he was unconscious, you put that awful stuff on your neck to make it appear Kyle had slit your throat."

"Yes ma'am."

"And then you stripped off his clothes—"

"No ma'am, Matty did that," Donny interrupted.

"And then you covered him with blood."

"Yes ma'am. Fake blood."

"And yourself."

"Yes ma'am."

"Then you put him in the bed, got in beside him, and when he awoke, pretended to be dead."

"Yes ma'am."

"So he'd think he'd killed you."

"Yes ma'am."

"All for what?" Lee accused. "For a joke?"

"That's what Matty said."

"And you never questioned it?"

"No ma'am."

Lee looked at me, then got up off the bed and walked into the bathroom. I heard the tap water run. Donny and I sat in silence until Lee returned, holding a washcloth to her head.

138

She reclaimed her perch on the bed, dabbing the cloth on her face.

"Aren't you ashamed?" Lee finally asked.

"No ma'am."

"What?" Lee reacted as if she'd been slapped.

"Ma'am," Donny's voice had dropped to a whisper, "if you knew some of the things I've done just to stay alive, you wouldn't even ask me that question."

Neither Lee nor I said anything. How could we possibly know what Donny's life had been like, the things he may have been forced to do just to survive. Sergeant Colbert had only intimated at some of the terrible possibilities. But here was this boy—living proof.

"What did you do then?" Lee's tone had softened.

"Then?"

"After Kyle woke up."

Donny inhaled deeply. "It was tough trying not to breathe. It wasn't so bad at first, because he went right into the shower. But when he came back out, I was supposed to stay very still until Matty returned." Donny smiled at me. "I tell you it seemed like forever. Then after Matty covered me with the sheet, I could breathe again."

"And after Kyle left?"

"Matty pulled the sheet off and told me I could go clean up."

"That's all he said?" I asked.

"He told me how great I'd done."

"Nothing else? No hint as to what this had all been about?"

"No sir. Except . . ." Donny paused.

"Yes?"

"He said something strange. Something I still don't understand."

"Yes?" This time Lee joined me in the chorus.

"Well, he said something about the balls in duchess court."

"Balls in duchess court?" I mimicked. "That doesn't make any sense."

"That's what I told you."

"Is that a place somewhere here in New Orleans?" Lee asked Donny.

He shook his head. "I never heard of it."

"Get the map that we picked up at the rental company," I instructed Lee. She walked over to the table and began sorting through several papers.

"This one?" she asked, holding up the map of the southwestern United States.

"No, no." I joined her at the table and started sifting through the various maps we'd collected. "Here's the one I mean," I said, holding up the trophy, "the one of New Orleans's city streets."

I scanned the index. "There's no Duchess Court," I admitted after checking three times.

"Maybe it's a park," Lee suggested.

"I looked. It's not a street, a park, or a landmark of any kind. Not in New Orleans. Or not on this map, at any rate."

"Maybe it's not a place then," Lee speculated.

"What do you mean?" I asked, folding the map and dropping it back on the tabletop.

"Did you ever see Hitchcock's *The Man Who Knew Too Much*?"

I nodded.

"Remember Jimmy Stewart when he's looking for Ambrose Chapel? At first he thinks it's a person and he makes a fool of himself at some pottery shop or something. Then Doris Day realizes it might be a place instead. And she goes off and finds the villains."

"Yes," I said, confused. "I remember. But what's your point?"

"Well, maybe the reverse is true here," Lee explained. "Maybe Duchess Court is not a place at all. Maybe it's a person."

"That'd be a funny name for a person," I commented.

"I've come across weirder names than that."

I nodded. "So have I. Let's try the phone book then," I said.

Lee flipped open the Greater New Orleans telephone directory. But after several minutes of scouting through both white and yellow pages, she shook her head. "There's no listing at all for anything called Duchess Court. It's not a person or a business." Frustrated, she slammed the book down on the table.

"Damn," I said. "Now what?"

Donny said nothing. He had offered no help at all while Lee and I had searched both map and directory. I had the uneasy feeling he knew more about Duchess Court than he was telling. But he wasn't talking.

Finally Lee broke the silence.

"I guess there's only one way to find out what it does mean," Lee finally offered.

"What's that?" I inquired.

"We'll just have to ask Matthew Hedges himself."

CHAPTER 15

"The novel paints a vivid and mesmerizing portrait of the fragility, the vulnerability, of innocence—a treasure so precious, so fleeting, that it's not truly appreciated until it's irretrievably lost."

—Stokes Moran,
on Thomas Tryon's The Night of the
Moonbow

The morning sun streamed through the parted draperies and pulled me from my dreams. As I returned to consciousness, I couldn't quite catch the fleeting images that darted just beyond my memory. Something about Seymour Severe. I had the vague certainty that in my dream I had put a face to the name, but I couldn't recall whose. Had it been Matthew Hedges? Or Manny Gillis? Or had it been the boy now stirring on the bed opposite me?

I moved cautiously. The chair at the room's writing table had not been designed for catching forty winks, and my muscles had grown stiff. Now my body screamed at the forced movement. I pushed myself up out of the chair and went to rouse Lee, who still lay in a seemingly comatose state on the other bed.

Lee and I had talked with Donny well into the morning

hours. The boy, once he had finished detailing his part in the implausible conspiracy, had proved surprisingly cooperative.

"And you're sure you don't have any idea who Seymour Severe is?" Lee had asked, for at least the third time, sometime around 3 A.M.

"No. I keep telling you, Matty never said a word. The first time I ever heard the name was when Matty told me Mr. Moran might be asking questions, and then he told me just what to say."

"Didn't that make you curious?" Lee persisted.

"Sure, but where Matty Hedges is concerned, I've learned it's sometimes better not to be too curious."

"What do you mean by that?" I asked.

Donny shrugged. "Sometimes it's just better not to know, that's all." The boy remained noncommittal.

"Come on," I insisted. "Tell me what that means."

"Well, it's just that Matty's involved in a lot of action." Yes, I thought, sex, drugs, who knew what else? "And he knows an awful lot of people."

"What kind of people?"

"Who knows? Maybe regular guys. Buttoned-down collars, black suits, slicked back hair."

"You mean Mafia?" I wasn't a mystery reader for nothing.

Donny laughed nervously. "No. I don't know. Like I said, maybe they're just regular johns." The boy clasped his arms around his chest and rocked forward. "But I also got the idea maybe they're not," he added.

"What makes you think that?" Lee inserted.

Donny continued his rocking motion. "I guess all the secrecy."

"Secrecy?" It was now my turn to prompt.

"Yeah. Most of the time Matty's a pretty up-front dude. But every once in a while he just drops outta sight and you won't see him for days at a time. Then when he comes back, he won't say a word about where he's been or what he's been up to."

"Have you asked?"

"Like I told you, ma'am, inquiring minds definitely don't want to know, not if they aim on staying healthy. I saw Matty angry once—just once—and that was enough for me. He almost killed a guy. Messed his face up real good. Matty's a martial arts expert, and he has a bad temper. No. I learned not to ask Matty too many questions, not if I wanted to keep my looks." He stopped rocking, then added almost shyly, "And without looks, I got nothing."

The naked truth of the boy's fragile life was revealed so simply, so honestly, that I almost cried. I wondered if Lee heard the same anguish, the same hopelessness in his voice. Or maybe I was just imagining it. After all, this was the life he had chosen. But how free had that choice been? Who knew what past wrongs had combined to create his present circumstances?

"So I'd be careful of Matty, if I was you," Donny continued, when neither Lee nor I had commented on his self-revealing admission. "He's not somebody to fool around with."

"Where can we find him?" I asked, then added, "Assuming we wanted to, that is."

"Matty's not easily found. Unless he wants to be."

"Doesn't he have an address or something."

"He lives somewhere in the Quarter is all I know. I've never been to his place, he's always come to mine."

I could hear the fatigue in his voice. Donny yawned. I

glanced at the travel clock on the nightstand. It was now nearly four.

"I think it's time to call it a night," I suggested. Donny nodded, curled into a ball on my bed, and fell quickly asleep.

"That's not exactly what I meant," I whispered to Lee after
she had spread a blanket over the slumbering boy.

She smiled. "Well, it won't hurt anything. And anyway, it
solves a problem for us. At least temporarily."

"What do you mean?"

"To tell you the truth, I haven't quite figured out what to do
with Donny. We really can't afford to have him running loose
where he can warn Hedges that we're here."

I nodded. "So what are we going to do?"

Lee yawned. "Right now, we're going to sleep. We'll worry
about that little problem later."

* * *

We had all slept in our clothes and, so, awoke stiff and wrinkled.
Lee was the first one into the bathroom. While she was changing, Donny talked idly of his past experiences. I was his audi-
ence, but I'm not sure he meant the conversation solely for me.
Maybe he just needed to get some things said for the record.

"You know, I was only ten when I first learned what sex was.
I had gone to a birthday party at a friend's house, and we were
playing hide-and-seek. I hid in this closet"—Donny stood at
the window and looked out toward the river—"and after a few
minutes, the door opened. I thought I'd been found. And then
the door closed, and I could feel somebody in there with me.

"I felt a hand go round my mouth, a big hand. And then the
other hand was pulling down my pants. I struggled, but he

had a powerful grip. Afterward, when the door opened again, I saw my friend's father leave the closet.

"I lay there the longest time, shivering, my pants still at my feet." Donny turned back toward me. He smiled. "That was my first time. Not anything to brag about, is it?" I shook my head and smiled back at him, wishing I could have been there, could have interceded, could have done something to stop the hurt. What I really wished was that I could do something now. But there wasn't anything I could do. This was his private burden, his excess baggage, and he'd carry it forever. Alone.

Lee emerged from the bathroom, looking radiant, and I nodded to Donny that it was his turn. I don't think I trusted my voice. Lee could tell something was wrong and asked me what it was. But I just shook my head. I'd tell her later. Maybe.

Feeling an overwhelming need to do something—anything—I found my voice, picked up the phone, and ordered a room-service breakfast for three.

"Have you thought of anything?" I asked Lee, remembering her "little problem" and realizing that we were getting close to a forced resolution.

"Not really," she acknowledged. "I think the best thing we can do is present our case to Donny and hope he goes along with it."

Which, when he emerged from the bathroom, is just what we did. But before Donny could respond, room service arrived with our breakfast order. After the waiter had been tipped and left, Lee reiterated her appeal.

"How much?" Donny asked, between mouthfuls of eggs and toast.

"What?" she asked.

NEIL McGAUGHEY

"I said, how much?" repeated Donny. "You don't expect me to keep quiet for nothing, do you?"

Considering what we had learned about him the previous evening, and what he had shared privately with me just a few minutes earlier, the boy's mercenary self-interest should not have come as any great surprise. But oddly, it did. Somehow I had gotten sucked into the fantasy that we were indeed a family. Donny's question dispelled that notion.

"What do you want?" I asked bluntly, strangely offended by his monetary gambit.

"Well, by this time, Matty knows I was picked up, and, with his connections, he probably knows why. Which won't come as any big surprise, since the first thing he asked me when we met—was I a runaway?" Donny had wolfed down his food in record time, while Lee and I still dawdled over ours. Now he pushed back his chair and stood up from the table. "You see, he still thinks I'm underage."

Donny paced while he talked. "Matty calls me jailbait." He smiled at the word. "So he won't take any risks trying to find me. When I don't show up for a few days, he'll just figure I'm back home with good old Mom and Dad."

The boy's logic made sense. Matty Hedges would indeed stay as far away from the situation as possible. A kid he believed to be a minor taken back by undoubtedly angry and outraged parents, Hedges would be a fool not to avoid it at all costs. And Donny was right about one other thing, too. Parents would not waste any time in taking their kid home. They wouldn't be like tourists on a sight-seeing junket. Which made me doubly glad we had avoided the French Quarter until the police business had ended.

"Which is not where I'll be." It took me a second for Donny's words to register that "home" was where he meant he wouldn't be. "But I sorta think a trip is just the ticket." Donny smiled. "I've always had a hankering to see L.A. And now's as good a time as any."

The boy's language—sometimes polished and even eloquent, other times crude and riddled with slang—reflected his confused personality. He paused, obviously waiting for our reply.

"How much?" Now Lee shot his own question back at him.

"Oh, five Benji's oughta do real fine."

"Five hundred dollars!" I translated the recently acquired lingo.

"I consider that a bargain," Donny postured. "After all, I'm willing to take the bus. I coulda hit you up for a plane ticket." He laughed.

Lee laughed with him. "Kyle, I think five hundred dollars is more than reasonable."

I shook my head. "I didn't say it wasn't. I just don't like the idea of paying him hush money. After all the recent mistakes I've made, I don't want to add another to the list." I made a decision. "Let him tell Hedges. It won't make that much difference. After all, we now know it was all a farce, anyway."

A worried frown crossed Lee's face. "Kyle, I think it would make a big difference. It would take away our one advantage—surprise. Come on, Kyle. We can charge it to expenses."

Back when Lee first hatched this plan, one way she had sold me on it was that *Playboy* would pick up the tab, if we nailed Severe. Right now, the way things were going, that remained a very big if.

"Oh, all right," I grudgingly agreed.

Lee reached for her purse, pulled out her billfold, and peeled off five "Benji's" from her horse-choking roll. Donny's eyes followed her actions closely. I hoped he wasn't getting any grander ideas.

Handing him the money, she said, "I trust you'll keep your side of the bargain."

Once again Donny smiled. "Lady, you ain't gotta thing to worry about." He folded the cash into a small rectangle, pulled off his right shoe, and stuck the money in the toe. "I guess I'll be on my way. Thanks for the chow, and the dough."

Lee interrupted his departure. "Kyle, why don't we take Donny to the bus station?"

"You don't hafta do that, ma'am."

Lee smiled sweetly at Donny. "I know we don't have to." She reached over and pinched his cheek. "We want to."

Just as I'd earlier played my part as Scrooge, now Lee was putting in her bit as Aunt Polly. I'm sure Donny did not make a gullible Tom Sawyer.

"How about my stuff?" Donny protested.

"What stuff?" Lee asked.

"Clothes, for one thing. I can't go to L.A. with just what I got on."

Lee reached again for her purse, pulled out the money roll, and peeled off another two hundred-dollar bills.

"Wouldn't you rather have some California threads?" she asked as she handed the money to Donny.

Donny again went through his fold-and-stash routine. When he had his shoe back on, he said, "Lady, you really do know how to speak my language. Next stop—L.A."

* * *

"You know, he can always turn around and come back," I commented.

"Or stop on the way and telephone," Lee added.

"This may sound strange, but for some reason I trust him."

"So do I."

Lee and I had watched Donny board the bus to Los Angeles, waited for it to pull away from the depot, and now stood alone on the tarmac where just minutes before had milled a throng of well-wishers and good-bye wavers.

I turned and faced Lee. "Are we doing the right thing?" I asked.

"What do you mean?"

"Maybe we should have tried to—I don't know—help him in some way."

"Kyle, he's twenty-two."

"I know. It's just he still seems like such a kid in so many ways."

Lee nodded. "He's had a tough life. He's probably somewhat emotionally retarded."

"It's just"—I didn't know how to express what I was feeling, so I lamely finished—"he got under my skin."

She smiled. "Mine too."

"And this is going to sound even stranger," I admitted, "but I'm going to miss him."

"Me too," said Lee, swiping at a loose hair on her forehead. Or was it a tear? "Just think. He'll probably be the only kid we ever have."

We both laughed as we darted from the protection of the

bus shed out into the pelting rain and made a hurried dash to the parking lot where we had left the Lincoln. In the couple of minutes it took to scamper the block and a half to the car, unlock Lee's door and then mine, we were both soaked to the skin.

"Now that we've got Donny taken care of, I think the first thing we should do—" Lee started.

"The first thing we're going to do," I interrupted, "is buy an umbrella."

CHAPTER 16

*"Readers unfamiliar with the lure and fasci-
nation of book collecting will find this mystery novel a delightful crash course on the
subject."*

—*Stokes Moran,*
on *John Dunning's* Booked to Die

The slightly off-key tinkling of the bell over the entryway
reminded me that I was once again at Murder on the Levee.
Lee and I had agreed, even though we believed Donny would
not betray us, that we needed to move fast. And we had further decided, after returning to the hotel from the bus station,
that our first order of business, after changing out of our wet
clothes, would be to beard the lion Manny Gillis in his den.

Now, standing on the fat man's threshold, I wasn't sure
what to do next. Lee nudged me and whispered to me to
browse. Which, in a bookstore, is something I don't need a
whole lot of encouragement to do.

I could easily spend hours here, lost in the company of
familiar friends. I stole a glance at the front desk, expecting to
see the bulk of Manny Gillis. But today a much thinner, much
prettier young woman sat behind the cash register. The big
man was nowhere in sight.

I ambled among the cases and finally stopped at a glass-

encased cabinet marked "Hardcover First Editions." I opened
the doors. My eye immediately lit on a much sought-after
prize. I pulled the vinyl-protected copy of Agatha Christie's
The Pale Horse down from the shelf. The dust jacket looked
fresh and new. I carefully opened the volume. It was a first edition, all right, and priced at a fairly reasonable seventy-five
dollars. I had to have this one, I decided, and stuck it under my
arm. Then I spotted an *"A" Is for Alibi* on the shelf beneath.

Five hundred dollars. Not bad, I thought. I'd seen this rare
title listed for as much as eight hundred and fifty. Not too far
away I found a copy of Jeremiah Healy's fine first novel, *Blunt
Darts*, listed for two hundred dollars. A little pricey, but who
was I to quibble.

Collecting mystery fiction can become an obsession. It's
definitely addictive, and I speak from firsthand experience. No
matter how many fine specimens you might have in your
library, it's always the ones you don't have that occupy your
thoughts. I collect mysteries because I love the genre, the stories, the writers. But for some people it's strictly a business.

For them, collecting is like investing in the stock market.
Some titles go up in value, some go down. Books by living
mystery writers are a chancier investment than those by dead
ones. A writer in demand today may be on the outs tomorrow.
A writer in disfavor today may be tomorrow's darling. You just
never know.

Most people think that age makes a book valuable. That's
not true. It's scarcity that's the true measuring stick. Small first
printings usually account for skyrocketing prices. Like everything else in our free trade economy, it's simply a question of
supply and demand. A fairly recent book, like Patricia D.

Cornwell's *Postmortem,* can easily sell for twice a fifty-year-old Ngaio Marsh.

I spied a copy of *Crocodile on the Sandbank* by Elizabeth Peters. I inspected it closely, comparing this three-hundred-and-fifty-dollar volume to the one I had purchased, some fifteen years before, for only a dollar. I smiled at my wise investment.

Admittedly though, at the time, I had not considered it an investment. It was just one of many mysteries I've purchased over the years from remainder houses. For the uninformed, a remainder is a book the publisher couldn't sell at full price and doesn't want to store. And if you're lucky enough to find a first edition without any telltale marking, such as inking or spraying, it will probably be your best chance at a real bargain. That's another definition of a collector—the bargain hunter. The smug feeling that you've pulled off some kind of coup. But outside of remainders, with the possible exception of garage sales, there aren't too many places these days where sellers don't know the true market value of the books in their inventories.

It wasn't too long ago when first editions of Dashiell Hammett's *The Maltese Falcon* or Raymond Chandler's *The Big Sleep* could still be found for under a hundred dollars. But alas, those days are gone, and today you could add two zeros to the amount and ten thousand dollars still wouldn't guarantee you a purchase.

So, as I traveled from one treasured volume to the next, I lamented the intrusion of big business into the world of collecting. I guess I'm old-fashioned. I believe a collector should acquire books he has an interest in, not books he thinks will appreciate in value. I collect books I like, books I want to keep forever. It makes me feel good to know a title I own is valued by other people, but the overriding factor for me remains enjoyment, not investment. I've bypassed mysteries by Ed McBain and Elmore Leonard, not because they were necessarily overpriced, but because I'd rather spend my money on a Dick Francis or a Julie Smith.

Thinking of one New Orleans writer put me in mind of another. I wondered what this city's asking price was for Anne Rice's *Interview with the Vampire*. Let's see how mercenary Gillis really is. I found the book in question and pulled it off the shelf. The gold dust jacket sparkled in the light. One thousand dollars. Pretty steep, but the fact that the book was signed by the author probably justified the exorbitant price. I replaced it with the indescribable self-satisfaction of knowing I had purchased a copy when the novel was brand new for the retail price of eight dollars and ninety-five cents. And my copy was signed too, now thankfully sitting safe and protected in my library back in Connecticut.

"Kyle, what are you doing?" Lee suddenly stood at my side.

I had been so engrossed in the books on display I had momentarily forgotten our reason for being here.

"Uh, just looking," I offered meekly.

"Well, we're not here to shop." She spotted the Christie under my arm. "Put that back. We don't want to buy anything."

"But wouldn't it look better for our cover—"

"No. Remember why we're here. Now put it back."

I reluctantly returned the cherished volume to its place on the shelf. I promised myself that no matter what happened, I'd be back to purchase the book.

"While you've been wasting time," Lee chastised, "I've been scouting around. There's no sign of Manny Gillis. And outside of you and me, the only other person in the store is the girl up front. Who shows absolutely no interest in anything except the book she's reading."

I peered around the First Edition case and saw that Lee was indeed correct. The young woman seemed entranced by Carolyn G. Hart's *The Christie Caper*. Which rekindled my sense of loss over *The Pale Horse*.

"There's a door over there, behind the girl and to the left." Lee nodded. "See it?"

"Yes."

"That must be the office. Manny Gillis may be in there. I want you to check it out."

"What?"

"I want you to check it out," Lee repeated, "while I distract the girl."

"I don't know," I said hesitantly.

"Do it," Lee ordered. "We don't have time to argue."

Lee walked to the front desk and engaged the young woman in conversation. I couldn't hear what was said, but after a minute, the girl closed the book she was reading and led Lee to the other side of the store.

I edged down the shelves toward the back wall. Lee had positioned herself so that the clerk was facing toward her, and away from me. I reached the door and slowly, quietly turned the knob. The door was not locked, and I cautiously looked into the room beyond. It appeared deserted. I eased through the entry, pulling the door closed behind me. I knew I had to hurry; Lee couldn't keep the clerk occupied for long.

I don't know that I've ever seen a more cluttered, more chaotic scene. Books covered every possible surface. The only light in the room came from a window high in the far wall. With the outside afternoon gloom offering little illumination, I chanced turning on the overhead light. I found the switch, and a startling 150 watts wiped away every shadow.

Not knowing exactly what it was I was looking for, I walked to the desk. At least fifty books littered its top, fighting a clock, a coffeepot, a calculator, and a half-eaten hamburger for space. I pulled against the center drawer, expecting it to be locked. It opened easily. It held an assortment of receipts, paper clips, pens and pencils. I tried the other drawers and found their contents to be much the same.

With the desk yielding nothing, I turned to the filing cabinet that stood against the back wall. It also was unlocked. The top drawer held billing files, publisher order forms, and client want lists. So too the second and third drawers. But when I pulled open the bottom drawer, I let out a gasp of surprise.

Raymond Chandler's *Farewell, My Lovely* slid into view. It was the American first edition, and both book and dust jacket were in mint condition. This priceless volume lay on top of a stack of about a dozen books. I carefully picked it up and laid it on the floor.

The next book in the stack was Dashiell Hammett's *Red Harvest*, followed in quick succession by Cornell Woolrich's *The Bride Wore Black*, Agatha Christie's *The Mysterious Affair at Styles*, S. S. Van Dine's *The Benson Murder Case*, John Dickson Carr's *The Three Coffins*, Rex Stout's *Fer-de-Lance*, Ellery Queen's *The Roman Hat Mystery*; Dorothy Sayers's *Murder Must Advertise* (the British first), another Chandler—

The Little Sister, another Hammett—*The Thin Man,* and James M. Cain's *Double Indemnity.* All with dust jackets, all in superb shape.

I was in collector's heaven. Here were some of the all-time classic mysteries, the cornerstones of the genre. You don't find these books anywhere anymore. And you certainly don't ever find them in such beautiful condition. But here they were, spread out around my feet. I had never before seen any of these titles in their first edition states. I calculated a conservative hundred thousand dollars for the lot.

As I lifted the last book from the drawer, I noticed a sheaf of papers underneath it. The papers were turned face down, so I had to slide my hand down to the metal bottom and scoop them out.

Before I saw the typed words on the top page, I knew I held in my hands a manuscript. And based on the other items from the drawer, I expected a gem. But I didn't quite expect the words "Untitled Novel, by Seymour Severe."

Here was the book only the publisher had seen. No review copies existed. No advance galleys. But this was not a publisher's copy. It was a typewritten manuscript—the original, or a carbon copy of the original. In Manny Gillis's filing cabinet. If this didn't make him Seymour Severe, I didn't know what did.

I heard a noise beyond the door, from the front of the store. I had no idea how long I'd been in the office. Too long, I was sure. I hastily stacked the priceless first editions back in the drawer and shoved it closed. But I kept the manuscript. My spur-of-the-minute decision surprised me, but it was the only proof I had—and I was not about to let it out of my hands.

The noise had not been repeated, and I had not been able

to identify it clearly. Some kind of crash, I thought. I stashed the loose manuscript under my coat, walked to the door, and eased it open. The clerk was on her hands and knees, picking up spilled books. Lee was offering profuse apologies. I edged out the doorway and sidled down the back aisle. Lee made a last apologetic gesture, left the clerk still straightening the tumbled-down display, and joined me at the entranceway. We stepped out into the damp New Orleans air.

"What took you so long?" Lee demanded. "I was running out of distractions."

"I guess I just lost track of time," I said, and then opened my coat and revealed the manuscript.

"What's that?" Lee asked.

"It's the new Seymour Severe mystery."

With Lee's mouth agape in astonishment, I added, somewhat redundantly, "I took it."

CHAPTER 17

"Four hours and change is all the time required to read it."

—*Stokes Moran,*
on Mary Higgins Clark's Loves Music,
Loves to Dance

"I still can't believe you stole that manuscript."

She wasn't the only one. My impetuous act continued to astound me, but at the time it had felt like the right thing to do. Now I wasn't so sure.

"I wouldn't call it stealing exactly," I countered.

"Oh really. Well, just what would you call it?"

"I dunno. Borrowing, maybe?"

"Sure. Try selling that to the cops."

Lee, mute throughout the long walk up Decatur to the Hilton, broke her silence with a vengeance as soon as the door to our hotel room had closed behind us. Her first words had been, "Are you crazy?" I shrugged and had then endured her repressed fury for the next several minutes. Now that the storm appeared to be abating, I said, "Don't you want to read it?"

Which started her up again. "Of course I want to read it. But just like everyone else. When it's between two covers and available at the local neighborhood bookstore."

"Suit yourself. But I'm not waiting." I picked up the four hundred or so loose pages, took them over to the reading table, turned on the lamp, and pulled out the chair, ready to read.

"Don't you realize that by taking that manuscript you've blown our plan?" Lee asked.

"I don't see how." I snatched a pillow off the bed, folded it over the back of the straight chair, and sat down, wiggling into a comfortable position.

"You don't think anybody will notice that it's gone?"

"Of course they will." I turned the cover page and started in on the first chapter. "But they won't know we took it."

"We didn't take it," Lee said sarcastically, "you did."

The next several hours passed without comment between us. Lee settled on the bed, watching television with the volume turned low. But she could have had the thing blaring for all I would have cared. Because I was lost in the fictional world of Seymour Severe and his erstwhile detective Giles Manning.

* * *

"Done," I said out loud as I dropped the final page on the heap of papers scattered across the top of the desk.

Lee offered no comment in return, concentrating instead on the comic antics of the Three Stooges. Moe yanked Curly's ears and ripped out some of Larry's hair. I stood up and stretched.

"I'm finished," I said, in case she had missed the import of my earlier pronouncement.

"Good," she said, with no inflection in her voice and without turning her head away from the television screen.

"Aren't you interested in my opinion?"

Lee clicked off the set and rolled to the edge of the bed, from which vantage point she eyed me assessingly. "Okay, Fingers, what's the score?"

She was trying for cynicism, but she didn't quite make it. The quiver at the edge of her lips gave her away, and we both laughed.

"Well," I said, relieved that the normal good feeling between us had been restored, "the book is vintage Severe. It has all the same qualities of his previous novels—strong characters, a dark and somewhat pessimistic view of humanity, lots of violence and sex. Plot's a little weak, though."

"But overall—" Lee left the question implied but unasked.

"Overall, it's as good as *The Bloodless Streets* and better than the other two. It should be a huge bestseller."

I walked to the window and closed the curtains. What had been a bleak December afternoon when I'd entered Severe's world was now a black New Orleans night. Only a few lights could be seen along the river.

"What are you going to do with the manuscript now?" Lee asked.

I turned to face her. "I'm going to keep it." I had not made the conscious decision to retain the manuscript until that moment. But I knew, at some time during my reading of the book, the line had been crossed.

"Kyle, you can't do that."

"Why not? I deserve something for everything they put me through," I asserted. I conveniently ignored the fact that I had willingly invited everything that had happened when I went looking for Seymour Severe.

"But it's not right."

"It is too right. It's the rightest thing I can think of. That manuscript is valuable. It's got Severe's own handwritten corrections penned in. You can call it my trophy, a keepsake of the fun they had at my expense."

"I'd think you'd want to forget that inglorious moment in your life, not memorialize it."

"Hell, I want to be reminded every day of my life what a fool I can be. I give it to them, they got me good. And now I've got them. I've got the manuscript."

"I can see there's no talking to you."

"Damn right," I said with conviction. "If they want it, they'll have to come and get it."

"I wouldn't be too sure they won't. Remember, you're dealing with dangerous people."

"They don't scare me. They've got me mad, and now they're the ones who better watch out for me."

"I've never seen you like this," said Lee.

"Well, you better get used to it. It's the new me."

"This may sound crazy, but I think I like you this way. You're more aggressive, more self-assured, more masculine. It's even a little sexy."

I let that last remark pass without comment. "I'm hungry," I suddenly realized.

"Me too," chorused Lee.

* * *

We ate in the hotel restaurant. Not a bad choice, but considering the world-class competition in the nearby French Quarter, definitely a comedown. But we had opted for convenience over gluttony.

"Well, one thing's clear—we now know for sure that Manny Gillis is Seymour Severe," I said between mouthfuls of Creole shrimp.

"Not necessarily," Lee said. "Severe could have just given him a copy of the manuscript to read." Then she added, "But it definitely proves a close connection."

"I think it does more than that. I think it proves Severe's identity."

"How can you be sure?"

"For one thing, I've met Gillis. You haven't. He's a book person. By trade and by choice. He's more likely to be Severe than Matty Hedges."

"Why?"

"Because Hedges didn't strike me as the literary type."

"Just what is the literary type?"

"I don't know. You. Me. Ernest Hemingway."

"How did Hemingway get into this?" Lee joked.

"You asked for a literary type. And he's the most literary type I know. Would you prefer Faulkner?"

Lee shook her head, and we ate in silence for a few minutes.

"Gillis and Hedges—are those our only two choices?" Lee asked, picking up the strand of our earlier conversation.

"The only two I know anything about. Tomorrow, we'll go back to the store and confront Gillis with our suspicions."

Lee frowned. "Not tomorrow we can't."

"Why not?" I asked.

"Because Gillis is out of town. That's something I learned from the clerk while I was trying to keep her distracted from your little excursion into the back room. He's off somewhere on a buying trip."

"When's he due back?" I choked down the last bite of food.

"She indicated he could be gone several days. According to her, his timetable is never too specific."

"Shit!" I picked up my cup of coffee. "That tears it. What are we going to do now?"

"There's always Matthew Hedges," Lee offered.

"Yeah. But where do we find him? Donny didn't help much in that regard."

"Perhaps we can make him find us," Lee said mysteriously.

"What do you mean by that?"

"Maybe it's time for Stokes Moran to make a return appearance."

"You mean I can get rid of this disguise."

"I don't see why not." Lee smiled. "It's served its purpose. Now that we know you didn't kill anyone, it's safe to be yourself again."

"Moran or Malachi—I'm not sure which is which anymore," I said matter-of-factly.

"That's good." Lee laughed. "Then neither will Hedges."

CHAPTER 18

"In this story, nothing is what it seems and no one is necessarily who they say they are or appear to be."

—*Stokes Moran,*
on William G. Tapply's The Marine Corpse

Getting rid of the mouthpiece, the body suit, and the contacts was a cinch compared to returning my hair color to normal. Mark Crews had given me a bottle of something he said would take the color right out. He was right. It took the brown out, but it didn't exactly restore the sandy blond.

After the first rinse, I looked like Elsa Lanchester in *The Bride of Frankenstein*. Three more intensive treatments got the color to a light brown, which I finally decided was as close as I would get, this side of a hair salon.

After a quick shower and a thorough blow-dry, I looked more like my old self, but I wasn't completely back to normal. My hair was still thin and not quite the original shade. But Lee pronounced me passable when I came out of the bathroom for the last time.

"Welcome back, handsome," she said, and planted a light kiss on my cheek, "I've missed you."

With only a towel wrapped around my midsection, I wasn't sure if this was the proper time or place. But I kissed her back. Full on the lips. Which started something of a ripple effect.

"I've missed you too," I said between kisses.

"It's about time," Lee whispered behind my left ear.

The towel dropped softly to the floor.

* * *

We awoke the next morning in the same bed. I opened my eyes and found Lee propped up on one elbow peering down at me. She smiled. I smiled back. The day could wait.

* * *

"What do we do first?" I asked as I pulled a sweater over my shirt.

"Why don't we do something detectives never try in mystery novels?" Lee suggested, gliding a slip down over her shoulders.

"What's that?" I asked.

"Look in the phone book."

Once again we tried the obvious. But I guess fictional detectives were pretty smart, after all. Just like Duchess Court earlier, there proved to be no listing for Matthew Hedges in the New Orleans directory. This time I slammed the book closed.

"Then I suppose we'll just have to see if we can't find Fido's." Lee snapped her skirt in place.

"But Donny said he didn't think it existed."

"Well, Hedges took you someplace. We'll see if we can't locate where that someplace is." She turned from the mirror. "And even if we can't find it, we need to get out, to see and be seen. Besides, a stroll through the French Quarter will finally give us a chance to sample some of that famous New Orleans cuisine."

Which is just what we found ourselves doing some thirty minutes later at an oyster bar on Royal.

"How far are we from where you were that night?" Lee asked between mouthfuls.

"I'm not exactly sure. I don't know the geography of the French Quarter well enough to pinpoint where we are now to where I was then." I sprinkled lemon juice on the slimy mollusk and let it slide down my throat. "We're only a street over from Bourbon so I wouldn't think it's more than four or five blocks."

Lee pushed back her plate, slurped her last drop of Louisiana chicory (which I can't stand, by the way), and said "Then let's find out."

I gulped down my last oyster and joined her at the cash register. She handed the proprietor a twenty-dollar bill.

"Let me do that," I protested.

"No it's fine. You can get the next one."

I nodded.

"And the one after that," Lee added. "And the one after that."

"Okay," I interrupted. "I get the idea."

We stepped out of the bar into the first bright sunlight I'd seen on either of my recent trips to the Big Easy. It was a refreshing counterpoint to the rain and gloom of the last couple of days.

I checked our current location. We stood at the corner of Royal and Toulouse. As we headed from Royal to Bourbon, I was amazed at the change in decor in less than a week's time. Six days ago the Quarter had been festively decked out for

Christmas. Now every vestige of that holiday had disappeared from view. I supposed this was the area's more normal guise, if anything about the French Quarter could ever be quite described as normal.

"Which way?" Lee asked at the intersection of Bourbon and Toulouse.

I tried to identify a landmark. "Left," I said blindly.

Bourbon Street remained Bourbon Street, twenty-four hours a day, three hundred and sixty-five days a year, no matter what the season, no matter what the occasion. The sex shops, bars, and restaurants all possessed that unique ambience found nowhere else in the world. I looked in one store window. The seasonal trappings were absent. The raunchy Santas had been replaced with plain nude mannequins, the dildos were now flesh-colored, and the other items had become even more outlandish—whips, chains, and exotic-looking vibrators were now prominently displayed. Maybe after Christmas, people got down to a harsher reality. I looked at the name of the establishment. High Boys. It was a T-shirt shop of all things.

Lee had walked on ahead. Now she paused and let me catch up with her.

"See anything interesting?" she smirked.

"Nothing that we need," I leered back.

We had walked two or three blocks down Bourbon when I noticed the Tail of the Cock restaurant on the far side of the street.

"This is about where I ran into Hedges that night. I think he was standing over there on that corner." I pointed to the spot. "But from there, I'm just not too sure. I wasn't paying close

170

OTHERWISE KNOWN AS MURDER

attention to where he was leading me, so I can't even tell you what direction we went from here."

We were now standing on the far corner.

"Well, let's just walk around and see if anything strikes you as familiar."

Lee and I veered off Bourbon and walked a couple of blocks down a side street. I kept on the lookout for a black wrought-iron fence, and I found several. But none looked right. And all seemed solidly attached to their moorings.

We walked back to Bourbon and headed off in the opposite direction. But with a similar lack of success.

When we found ourselves standing on the corner across from the Tail of the Cock for the third time, I said, "Let's give it up. We're not going to find anything this way."

"I guess I was just naive," Lee admitted. "Somehow or other I thought if we just got you here, you'd have no trouble finding the place. But I guess it doesn't work like that."

"It was worth a try," I consoled.

"Okay," Lee bounced back, "what now?"

"I suppose the only thing left for us to try is to go to the Queen Royale and see if we can spot Hedges there."

* * *

After sitting in the elegant lobby of the hotel for more than three hours, and visually inspecting every male who passed through, I conceded defeat, and told Lee as much. She nodded her head in agreement.

"We'll just have to let him find us," she said, as we stood to leave.

"Wait. Let me try one other possibility." I walked to the

desk. The clerk on duty did not look familiar to me, but over the years I had relegated all service people to virtual invisibility. You might recall every detail about a man who mugged you, but waiters and clerks became almost indistinguishable one from the other. But I doubted if I was the only person who suffered from such occupational blindness.

"Yessir?" the man behind the counter asked.

"I wonder if you can help me."

"Certainly. If I can."

"Do you know a man named Matthew Hedges?" The clerk shook his head.

I then described Matthew Hedges to him as best I could.

"I'm afraid not," he responded. "Hundreds of people come in and out of this lobby every day. I may have seen a man dressed all in white recently, but then, maybe not. You'd think I'd remember that, though, wouldn't you?" He grinned at me. "But believe me, we get a lot more unusual dress in here than that."

"Thank you anyway," I said, and turned to leave. I suddenly realized that I'd be hard-pressed to recall the features of the clerk to whom I'd just been talking. I spun around and pointedly registered his appearance in my mind. I guess anonymity was just a hazard of the trade.

"Any luck?" Lee asked when I had returned to her side.

"No," I grumbled.

"Any other bright ideas?"

"Not really."

"Well, it's still early. Do you mind if we mix a little business with our pleasure? My business, I mean."

"What are you talking about?"

"Well, you remember the call I made from your house on Christmas Eve? To New Orleans?"

I nodded. "The romance writer," I said.

Lee frowned. "Now don't start."

I lifted my hands in mock surrender, certain that a "Who me?" expression was clearly etched across my face.

Lee continued. "Well, she is a client, and she lives right here in the French Quarter. It wouldn't inconvenience us much, and she did help you out, after all, getting that information on Donny," Lee argued. I nodded assent, but she was intent on further justifying her case. "And I'd hate for her to find out I was down here and didn't let her know. Or drop by. Or something. You know what I mean?" Lee smiled. "Kyle, is that all right with you?"

"It's fine with me." I laughed. "Just as long as we don't go into the real reason why we're here. The fewer people who know that the better." Lee nodded agreement. "But since we have nothing else to do right now, at least one of us ought to try and salvage something out of this wasted day."

"Great." Lee gave me a peck on the cheek. "Let me call and see if she's home. I'll be right back."

* * *

The address to which Lee led me was not far off Bourbon. The house exuded elegance and charm. It had a red brick front and black wrought-iron balconies in the French architectural style common to the Quarter. We passed under the portico and Lee tapped the knocker against the massive wooden door.

"Yes?" A uniformed butler answered our summons.

"Lee Holland to see Miss Prescott."

"Follow me." The man swung the door wide, allowed us to enter, closed the door behind us, and escorted us into what had to be the library. The room was filled floor to ceiling with shelves bulging with books. The only break in the walls were three French windows through which could be seen an expansive courtyard.

"I'm impressed," I said, as I surveyed the room. "What a collection!"

"Yes. I'm sure—" But before Lee could tell me what she was sure of, she was interrupted by the arrival of a white-haired elderly woman dressed all in scarlet. Scarlet dress, scarlet shawl, scarlet slippers. Even her face looked scarlet. It looked as if she had stepped right out of a game of Clue. Here she was, Miss Scarlet. In the library. And I wondered if she had recently killed anyone—perhaps with a lead pipe? Or was it a lead wrench? I couldn't remember the game well enough to correctly recall which it was.

"Lee, what a pleasant surprise. I had no idea you were in town. You didn't say a word about coming down when I talked to you on the phone the other evening." The lady gestured a kiss in the general direction of Lee's right cheek. "I'm afraid I haven't come up with anything else on that bellboy you asked me about."

"That's all taken care of," Lee answered curtly, then she turned toward me. "Agatha, I'd like you to meet Kyle Malachi. Kyle, this is Agatha Prescott." I acknowledged the introduction, somewhat embarrassed by my belated recognition. I should have realized the minute Lee asked for Miss Prescott whom she meant. Agatha Prescott—the world-famous romance novelist. In the flesh. Author of more than fifty best-selling novels over the past fifty years. A living legend. No wonder Lee had been so upset over my put-downs. Agatha Prescott was clearly in a league by herself.

"It's a pleasure, Mr. Malachi." She held my hand, and I could see a sparkling energy in those violet eyes.

"Kyle's a client of mine too, and you might know him by his pen name—Stokes Moran?"

Agatha let out a sound that can only be described as a yip. "Yes indeed. The mystery critic. I read your reviews every Sunday in the *Picayune*." The New Orleans newspaper, the *Times-Picayune*, has subscribed to my syndicated column for the past three years.

"Let's all sit down. Mr. Malachi, or should I say Mr. Moran?"

"Just call me Kyle."

"And you call me Agatha," she countered. "Kyle, come sit beside me." She indicated an overstuffed sofa in the center of the room. Lee perched on an identical sofa facing Agatha and me.

"Would you care for some tea?" asked Agatha after we were all comfortably settled.

"No thank you," Lee and I said in virtual unison. The three of us laughed.

"Well, how about some brandy?" Agatha tried again.

"No, nothing," Lee answered, and I shook my head in agreement.

"Well, what brings you to New Orleans at this time of year?"

"Kyle and I had some estate business to take care of."

Estate business? Where was Lee heading with this one? "Kyle's uncle died recently—"

"Oh, I'm so sorry," Agatha said to me, reached out and patted my hand. I smiled.

Lee continued, "—and he had to come down here to close up his uncle's affairs. So I just decided to come along too." Lee's imagination never failed to astonish me.

"I'm so glad you did. I was going to call you tonight. This new contract my publisher sent me is just so confusing. Are you sure it includes all the points we discussed?"

"I think so. I ironed it out with Dale"—Lee turned to me and explained—"Dale is Agatha's editor." Then she looked back to Agatha. "As I was saying, I ironed everything out with Dale after you left town last month. Is there a problem?"

"You know me. Anything legal just gets me all boggled. Would you mind going over it with me again?" Agatha asked sheepishly.

"Not at all."

"It's in my writing room upstairs." She turned to me. "Mr. Malachi—Kyle—would you mind terribly if I took this lovely lady away from you for a minute?"

"Not at all." We all stood.

"Make yourself at home."

"I was noticing your library," I angled.

"Then feel free to browse to your heart's content," Agatha offered. "I think you'll find I have some pretty nice selections."

The two women left me alone with perhaps five thousand books. I started with the shelf beside the mantel. Histories and biographies. I moved to my right. True crime. I turned to the adjoining wall. Romantic fiction, with four long shelves holding what I assumed were the collected works of Agatha Prescott. Including foreign printings. The next shelves held regional fiction—Eudora Welty, Walker Percy, William Styron. I lifted a few volumes down from their places. All first editions. All personally inscribed.

This collection must be worth a fortune, I assessed. I walked across the room to the shelves along the far wall. Ah, mysteries. At last. Works by Christie, Sayers, Dick Francis, Simon Brett, Elizabeth Peters. Books I had been scouting for years, without success. *The Curse of the Pharoahs. Cast, in Order of Disappearance. Odds Against.*

Every mystery writer I could think of was represented. All first editions, and many of these inscribed as well. I noticed one of my favorites—*The Affair of the Bloodstained Egg Cosy* by James Anderson. A marvelous novel in the Christie tradition. Here were also *The Last Good Kiss* by James Crumley, *Yellow-Dog Contract* by Ross Thomas, *A Little Class on Murder* by Carolyn G. Hart, *Corpse in a Gilded Cage* by Robert Barnard, and many other to-die-for prizes. This was a more complete collection than any I'd ever before encountered. Agatha obviously had very eclectic tastes. Or a lot of friends. I would kill for a treasure like this.

On a shelf halfway up the wall, I spotted the three Seymour Severe novels. I pulled down *Dreamers Die Dirty* and flipped to the copyright page. It too was a first edition. I leafed back to the front endpaper.

At first I couldn't believe what I was seeing. As far as I knew, there were no signed Seymour Severes anywhere in existence. But this book was not just signed, it was inscribed. And it was the words that had me in shock: "To Mother, with all my love." And then the name, with a noticeable flourish, "Seymour Severe."

The handwriting looked vaguely familiar, and I tried to place it. Of course, the markings on the manuscript I had taken from Murder on the Levee. Could Manny Gillis be Agatha Prescott's son? It didn't seem likely. For one thing, his age.

I heard the women coming back down the stairs, so I hastily returned the book to its rightful place. I moved to greet Lee and Agatha.

"Well, Kyle, are you about ready to go?" Lee asked.

"If you are," I answered. As the three of us walked into the entryway, I turned to Agatha and asked, "By the way, do you have any children?"

A perplexed look crossed her face. "As a matter of fact, I have two. They're both grown now, of course."

"A son?" I continued.

"Yes. Matthew."

"Matthew Hedges?" I could feel Lee tense beside me.

"Yes, again. Do you know him?"

"Just casually," I said, as Lee and I took our leave.

* * *

"What a remarkable discovery," Lee said as soon as the mansion door had shut behind us.

"I still can't believe it."

"How did you come up with it?"

I explained about the book's inscription. Then I had another thought. "Let's walk around this block," I said to Lee.

We rounded the corner and moved halfway down the street,

until we came to a narrow opening between buildings. Bridging the opening was a wrought-iron grille.

I stopped. "Lift up, right there in the middle," I directed Lee. She did as I instructed, and the railing opened inward. A gate. She looked at me in consternation.

I was certain this passageway would lead directly into the courtyard I had glimpsed from Agatha Prescott's library.

I had found Fido's.

CHAPTER 19

"But through it all, the hero survives—a little older, a little more cynical, a little less alive. The recent events in his life have taken their toll."

—*Stokes Moran,*
on Charles Willeford's The Way We Die Now

"But yesterday, you were just as certain that Manny Gillis was Severe."

"And now I'm positive it's Matthew Hedges."

"Just because of that inscription?"

"Just because of that inscription. What else do I need?"

"Someone could have written that in the book for any number of reasons."

"Name one."

"As a joke, maybe. Who knows?"

"A joke?"

Lee and I had carried on a heated dialogue since leaving Agatha Prescott's house. Now, back in our hotel room, we were still debating the issue.

"Okay, say you're right," Lee said. "That Matthew Hedges is indeed Seymour Severe. Where does it get you? Hedges is never going to admit it, or agree to an interview. And no matter what you say, *Playboy* is never going to go with the story without absolute proof."

"I think that inscribed book is absolute proof," I argued. I walked to the bureau, opened the top drawer, and lifted Severe's manuscript out and handed it to Lee. "And this is proof too. The handwritten margin notes match the handwriting in Agatha Prescott's copy of *Dreamers Die Dirty.* Don't tell me that's not corroboration. I've read enough mystery novels to know that's more than enough."

Lee laid the manuscript down beside her on the bed. "This doesn't prove anything," she said. "Without the book to compare the handwriting to, you've still got nothing."

"Then I'll get the book."

"Kyle," Lee warned.

"What?"

"If Hedges is Severe, Agatha will never give you that book. They'll know you're trying to expose him. Surrendering that book is the last thing he'd let her do."

"Who said anything about surrendering?"

"Kyle," Lee warned again.

"Look, I already took the manuscript. What's a little more larceny among friends?"

"These aren't your friends. They're dangerous." Lee stood up and took my hands. "You're not thinking about doing something really stupid, are you? Like breaking into that house?"

I pulled my hands from hers. "Look what they already did to me. Don't you think that gives me the right to go after them?"

"Yes, to a degree. But not to the point of committing a

felony. Look, you've already stolen the manuscript. I can't believe you're seriously considering this." Lee's voice was harsh. "You're pushing your luck. You could get thrown in jail."

"I don't care. I'll just have to take that chance." I walked over to the window, parted the curtains, and looked out into the dimming twilight. It had started to rain once again. "I'm going back there tonight. Late. Maybe an hour or so before dawn, when I can be pretty certain everyone will be asleep."

"That's breaking and entering. Kyle, please don't do that," Lee pleaded. She joined me at the window and tried to turn me toward her. I resisted.

"My mind's made up," I said, finally turning to face her.

"You don't know what you're suggesting. You could get hurt," she pleaded.

"I can take care of myself," I asserted.

"No you can't, you big dumb asshole." Was that irritation or panic in her voice? "All you know how to do is read and write. You're totally out of your depth in the real world. You've lived in your protective cocoon so long you don't know anything else. You think just because you've read action thrillers, you can live action thrillers. Well, I have news for you. You're not James Bond."

"Try Sam Spade." I took her hands and smiled.

"No, not Sam Spade either." But Lee was smiling now too.

"Then Miss Marple will have to do."

We both laughed, then hugged. When we broke the closeness, Lee stated, "I see there's no talking you out of this."

I shook my head.

"Then I'm going with you."

"Oh no. No you're not. You're staying right here."

"If you can be Sam Spade, I can be Vic Warshawski."

"Warshawski gets beat up a lot," I said. "I'm not going to put you in any jeopardy." I pulled her back in my embrace. "Now that I have you, I'm not going to let anything happen to you."

"Don't you think I feel the same way?" Lee argued. "Let's just forget the whole thing and go back home. We've accomplished most of what we came here to do."

"No, I'm not leaving here until Hedges, Gillis, and whoever else may have been in on this little scheme realize I'm very much their equal."

"Kyle, I never thought I'd see you fall into macho bullshit."

"Call it anything you like. I'm playing it all the way to the end."

"But, Kyle, you might be their intellectual equal." I frowned, and Lee quickly amended, "I mean, you are their intellectual equal. Probably even their intellectual superior. But this is not a mental exercise. Look at what they did to you. They play mean, and dirty." Lee pulled me onto the bed. "You don't know how to fight in their arena."

"Then I think it's just about time I learned."

* * *

The travel alarm sounded at 3 A.M. At first, in the fogginess of sleep, I thought a bee buzzed around my head. Slowly, consciousness returned, and I reached over to the nightstand and tapped the buzzer off. Lee slept quietly at my side.

I quickly slipped into my clothes. No shave and shower were needed for breaking and entering, I decided.

* * *

The water-slicked streets shone with reflections from the lights of the city. It was oddly still at this early morning hour. The rainstorm from earlier in the evening had diminished to little more than a fine mist. I walked the streets virtually alone.

As I approached the block where Agatha Prescott lived, I began to have second thoughts. Maybe Lee had been right. Maybe this was a foolish thing to do. But as I stood in front of the wrought-iron fence, all doubts deserted me. I lifted up on the railing, pushed it open, and entered the dark and narrow alley.

It was not as pitch black as on my previous nighttime excursion here. But the alley still offered little illumination, and I had to move cautiously. Suddenly the enclosed courtyard opened up in front of me, and for the first time I gave thought to the mechanics of accomplishing my mission. I had brought no tools with me, no means with which to force an entry.

I identified what I thought were the windowed doors to the library and eased toward them. I didn't want to knock over a planter or chair and herald my presence. I made it to that side of the house without incident.

And luck was with me. The first glass door I tried opened silently at my touch. Trusting souls, I thought. I edged through as small an opening as I thought safe and found myself indeed in the same room I'd occupied several hours earlier. I carefully closed the door behind me, letting the latch catch with no sound whatsoever.

As expected, the room was dark. But enough light shone through the windows to allow my eyes to adjust to the dimness. It didn't take long before I could even make out some of the book titles on the shelves.

Now where were the Severes? I located the bookcase housing the mystery novels. Had they been on the third shelf or the fourth?

I heard a noise from the front of the house. I paused, my heart in my throat. What had it been? Just a sound a house makes in the middle of the night? Or was it a telltale warning of someone else afoot?

The noise did not come again, and my heartbeat slowly returned to reasonable limits. I once again directed my attention to finding the inscribed Severe.

I made out a book title. *The Last Camel Died at Noon.* Had Severe been on the same shelf as Elizabeth Peters? Possibly. I vaguely remembered coming across Peters before Severe. Maybe the books were arranged in alphabetical order. I strained my vision farther down the shelf.

Dreamers Die Dirty. There it was! I reached to take the volume in my hands. I heard rather than felt the thump. But I instantly knew what it was. A blaze of lightning flared behind my eyes, then a spinning redness reached out for me, until finally I slipped into a bottomless black hole.

* * *

A bloodied Matthew Hedges chased me down the never-ending alley. Disembodied corpses impeded my path. I jumped body part after body part. Here an arm, there a leg. Rolling hideous heads. I was running an obstacle course of horror.

I looked back. Hedges was gaining on me, clutching a gleaming butcher knife in his hands, hacking away at the empty air, making a hideous sound in his throat, laughing through the scarlet ooze that seeped from the gaping hole in his neck.

It was the laughter that brought me around. I forced my eyelids open and painfully focused on the man standing slightly above me. Yes, he was laughing all right. His round belly shook with the effort. No, it was not Matthew Hedges, but rather Manny Gillis who greeted my astonished eyes.

"How nice to see you again, Mr. Moran," he said, after his laughter subsided. "Or should I say, Mr. Malachi?"

How did he know my real name? "Either one will do," I responded. My voice sounded muffled in my ears.

He laughed again. "I'm happy to hear you still have your sense of humor."

"I never lost it."

"Never say never, Mr. Malachi. You just never know what the future may hold."

I took his comment for the implied threat it was. Since I didn't feel like carrying the banter any further, I tried to stand. But my hands and feet were tied to the chair. I rested my head back against the cushion and surveyed the scene. I recognized the room. There in front of me was the curved, elevated runway. Fido's.

"Where's Hedges?" I asked.

"Oh, he's around and about. In fact, I expect him back any minute. He had a little errand to run."

I heard a noise behind me. Feet slapping against the polished hardwood floor.

"Here he is now," Gillis said. "And how nice, he's brought company."

Then Lee was suddenly propelled into my line of vision.

CHAPTER 20

"But when he does call it a wrap, the detective does so with a flair for the dramatic that would have made Shakespeare proud."
—*Stokes Moran,*
on Caroline Graham's Death of a Hollow
Man

"Kyle, are you all right? They haven't hurt you, have they?" Lee stood beside me and cupped my face in her hands.

"I'm okay, Lee." She had warned me against this folly, and now I had placed both our lives in jeopardy. "I'm sorry I got you mixed up in this."

"Forget that." I could see the anger in her eyes. Like a mama bear protecting her cub, she turned on Manny Gillis. "What did you do to him?" Lee shrieked.

"Just gave him a little conk on the head." The voice came from behind me, and a little to my left. Then a man walked into my limited sight circle. It took me a minute to realize it was Matthew Hedges. Gone was the man in white; tonight he wore an open-necked turquoise sweater over khaki slacks.

"Untie him," Lee demanded. "You've got him trussed up like some kind of animal."

Hedges nodded to Gillis, who walked over, knelt to release my leg restraints, then moved behind the chair and untied the ropes binding my hands. I pulled my arms from behind me and rubbed the circulation back into my wrists.

Gillis returned to his perch against the raised runway. The pecking order had been established. Matthew Hedges was clearly the one in charge.

Lee sat in my lap, put her arms around me, and cradled my head against her chest. I felt her finger the goose-egg behind my right ear.

"Ouch."

"You are hurt." Lee pulled back.

"It's nothing," I said. "You were right. I should never have come here. I got myself in trouble, and you too."

"It's a little late for regrets," Hedges said.

"Yeah," I said, then spoke to Lee. "What are you doing here? Did you follow me?"

"No. This brute"— she stressed the word, inclining her head toward Hedges—"showed up at the hotel and told me you'd had an accident."

"He didn't hurt you, did he?" Suddenly I was angry, more at my colossal stupidity than anything else.

Hedges laughed. "I was the perfect gentleman."

"How did you know where to find her?"

"Like I told you on your last visit, I know everything."

"Matty, what's going on?" Agatha Prescott swept into the room, aswirl in blue silk. "Lee? Kyle? What are you doing here?"

"Mr. Malachi paid us an unexpected visit, Mother." Like Gillis earlier, Hedges called me by my real name. I was beginning to believe in his claimed omniscience. "You might say he crashed the party." Hedges grinned.

"Very clever," Lee said sarcastically.

"What your son means," I continued, "is that I broke into your house tonight."

Agatha gasped. "Whatever for?" she asked.

"This afternoon, when you and Lee left me alone in the library, I came across your inscribed copy of *Dreamers Die Dirty.* I came back to steal it." It sounded awfully criminal when I said it like that.

Agatha's response surprised me. "Oh" is all she said. Then she turned to Hedges. "This has gone on long enough. It's time we brought it to a halt."

"I agree, Mother," Hedges said. He scanned the faces in the room, waiting expectantly for something. After a minute, he added, "Well, I suppose it's up to me to be the narrator."

Hedges pulled out a chair and sat across from me and Lee.

"Mr. Malachi—may I call you Kyle?" Not on your life, buddy, I thought. His friendly attitude confused me.

"I was cast as the villain," he said. "Not that I minded, of course. I kinda like playing the bad guy. After all, I'm not exactly what you'd call a saint."

"You can say that again," his mother interjected.

Hedges smiled. "So it was up to me to set everything in motion."

"I don't understand," I said. I felt like I'd entered the middle of a conversation. "Set what in motion?"

"Let's call it—the Get Kyle Malachi Caper."

"Don't you mean Stokes Moran?" I asked.

"Oh no." He smiled again, rising from his seat. "Let's get the whole cast of characters out here on stage." Taking his cue, emerging from the shadows at the right end of the runway, stepped Donny. Back from L.A.? At this moment, nothing seemed to make sense. Strangely, I was glad to see him, and the boy—for that's how I still thought of him—sent me a friendly salute.

"Good." Hedges turned back to me. "Now that we're all assembled, I can tell you. Kyle Malachi, you've been had."

He laughed. "You were going to play the great detective. Come swaggering down here and unmask the mysterious Seymour Severe. Well, that's about to happen. The reclusive author is here with us right now."

I looked from face to face. Was Seymour Severe in this room right now? If so, who could he be? At one time or another, I had considered, rejected, then reconsidered just about everyone here. Manny Gillis? I had suspected him when I'd discovered the manuscript in his office. Donny? No, he was too young to have written the books. Agatha Prescott? She had the talent to do it, and the track record, as her dozens of best-selling novels could attest. But her writing was so different in tone and content, it didn't seem possible that she could also be the author of the sexy and violent thrillers. Seymour Severe belonged to the hard-boiled school, in the same league as Hammett and Chandler. No, Agatha wasn't the type.

Which brought me back to my prime suspect—Matthew Hedges. He had always seemed to be the one pulling all the strings from the start.

Hedges had paused in his monologue, giving me time, I supposed, to consider all the possibilities. "Isn't this fun?" he commented after a minute. "Right out of the classic mystery scenario. All the suspects gathered together for the unveiling." He began to walk the room. "But with one important difference. And, Kyle, do you know what that difference is?"

I shook my head.

"Well, I'll tell you. This time the tables are turned. The great detective is not the one doing the unmasking. As a matter of fact, the great detective is a miserable bust." He smirked.

"I agree," I said.

"Not only are you not Sherlock Holmes or Nero Wolfe, you're not even Dr. Watson or Archie Goodwin."

He had me there.

"Your abilities remind me more of something out of a Hercule Poirot novel. But not the little Belgian. No, Kyle, you get the Arthur Hastings part." If nothing else, Hedges was proving he was well read. And he was right. I indeed felt like the bubble-headed Poirot sidekick Christie had discarded after a few novels for being too stupid and too dense.

"As Poirot would say—ah, my dear Hastings, you are the fool."

During this discourse, Gillis, Donny, and Agatha had remained mute. Now Agatha spoke up. "Matty, will you please get on with it. I think you're enjoying the tease too much."

"All right, Mother," Hedges said. Lee clutched my hand. Was this the moment we'd anticipated? Had it finally come? Were we about to discover the true identity of Seymour Severe? I squeezed Lee's hand in return—for encouragement, for hope, for success.

"Maybe I am having too much fun at Kyle's expense. But just look at the poor bugger. He hasn't a clue."

"Get on with it," Agatha repeated. The terseness in her voice made me momentarily reconsider my earlier rejection of her as Severe. Maybe she does possess the toughness, I amended.

Hedges sat in the chair once again. "Kyle, I had two things to accomplish. One, I was to make sure you were not homosexual."

"Why?" I demanded.

"Patience, my dear Hastings. To quote Poirot again, all will be revealed. There'll be time for questions later," he offered.

"Now the method I was to use"—Hedges picked up the previous thread of his narrative—"was pretty much left up to me." He laughed. "And perhaps I did get a little bit too theatrical with it, but then I'm not known for my subtlety. And my script did achieve its purpose. I established that you were not gay. More's the pity," he leered at me. "The times we could have had."

He patted my knee. "But I digress." Hedges tilted back in his chair, bringing it to rest against the elevated runway.

"Now I'm sure you've been wondering exactly how I did it. Well, for one thing, and I do apologize for this, I did rely just a little bit on chemical substances. But I can assure you the drug I slipped you that night was not a Mickey."

"Then what was it?" I asked.

"Just a little something of my own invention. And you're asking questions again."

I shrugged an unfelt apology.

"You must have a very low tolerance for drugs. The intended effect was supposed to reduce your defenses, to overcome your inhibitions, and to allow you to freely indulge in your natural desires. Instead, you passed out.

"But never, in any of your moments of rare consciousness,

did you demonstrate the least interest in any members of your own sex." He grinned again.

"Will you stop prolonging this? I want to get back to bed." Agatha's impatient irritation with her son was clearly evident.

"Mother, I'll relinquish center stage in just a minute." Hedges snapped forward and brought the chair legs back flat to the floor.

"So that was number one. And I must say, I accomplished my objective in record time." He winked at me.

"Now, number two was a different matter entirely," he said, then paused. "But wait. Why don't I let Mr. Severe tell you all about number two?" Hedges stood up.

"Well," he said, when no one immediately responded, "don't you want to take it from here, Mr. Severe? Now's your chance. Better speak now or forever hold your piece." He grinned.

No one moved. The atmosphere in the room was almost electric. I tensed for the long-anticipated revelation. It was quick in coming.

"Number two," Lee said, "was to send you into my arms."

CHAPTER 21

*"And in the end, body a little bruised and ego
a little battered, he triumphs. And so does the
reader."*

—*Stokes Moran,
on Jesse Sublett's* Tough Baby

"You're Seymour Severe?" Of all the things I could have said
at that moment, that was perhaps the most ridiculous. But
those were the words I voiced.

Lee slipped her hand out of mine. "Yes," she said. "I'm
Seymour Severe."

I couldn't believe it. With my senses still reeling, my vocab-
ulary failed me. "Why?" is the best I could come up with.

Lee misunderstood my question. "I wrote the first book
when I was twenty-four. That was almost fifteen years ago. Before Sara Paretsky and Sue Grafton. Just about the same time
Marcia Muller came out with *Edwin of the Iron Shoes.*" Muller's
first novel is generally regarded as a landmark in women's
mystery writing—the first distaff hard-boiled novel. "But my
book," Lee continued without interruption, "was much gritti-
er, much more violent. Can you imagine at that time any publisher gambling on *The Bloodless Streets* by a woman author?

"So I came up with a pseudonym—Seymour Severe. And
the rest, as they say, is history."

Lee stood up and walked over to Matthew Hedges.

"You didn't have to hit him. That wasn't in the script." I could hear the anger in her voice.

"How was I to know who it was? I came home late; I heard somebody in the library; I looked in and saw this shadow at the shelves; so I conked him. It wasn't until he was out cold and I turned on the lights that I knew who I'd bashed." He seemed offended at her criticism. "And why didn't you alert us he'd be coming?"

"I tried. And kept getting a busy signal."

"Mother?" Hedges asked. "Did you take the phone off the hook again?"

Agatha smoothed the blue silk around her legs, training her eyes on her feet. "You know I hate having my sleep disturbed by that stupid telephone," she said.

Lee ignored Agatha's complaint. "But why tie him up? That certainly wasn't called for."

"I thought it added a little verisimilitude," Hedges grinned. "Anyway it kept him on ice until you could get here."

Lee turned her back on him, pulled out another chair, sat down, and faced me.

"Kyle, let me start from the beginning."

"I wish you would," I said. Now that the shock was beginning to wear off, I could feel the first stirrings of anger. It was finally beginning to sink in that the author of my humiliation was my own agent.

"In case you haven't figured it out, Agatha Prescott is my mother and Matthew Hedges is my brother."

"Yes, that's right," Agatha interrupted, finally looking up

from the floor. "Lee is a result of my third marriage to Mr. Holland. Perfectly dreadful man. Ate cashews in bed. Crunch crunch, crunch crunch. All the time. Awful man, just awful." I caught the tolerant smile lurking behind Lee's eyes.

"Matthew here came from my second. Marriage, that is. His father was killed in Korea. We'd only been married a month. I didn't have time to find out if he had any bad habits."

Agatha conversed as if at a mid-afternoon tea party. "My first husband was Mr. Prescott. We married right after the war—excuse me, World War II, that is—which will always be The War for people of my generation. Now where was I?"

"Mother." Lee sighed and sent her mother an exasperated look.

"Oh yes," Agatha continued, "I caught him cheating on me in '48. Or was that '47? No matter. Messy divorce. But I had already published two books, and I couldn't very well change my name." She turned toward me. "I know you understand, Kyle. I was just like poor Christie—stuck with the name of a man I hated."

"Mother." Lee attempted to derail the steam locomotive that was Agatha Prescott on a roll.

"All right, dear. I was just trying to fill Kyle in on our family history." Some family, I thought. "Now where was I? Oh yes. My maiden name—isn't that such a quaint expression— maiden name. It sounds like something that should come with a chastity belt." Agatha spotted the frown on Lee's face. "Well, my maiden name is Gillis, and Manny here is my baby broth- er." She blew him a little kiss.

"I guess that covers everybody." Agatha scanned the room.

"Except the boy. He's not related to anybody that I know of. I don't even know what he's doing here." Donny cast his eyes to the floor.

Matthew Hedges interrupted, anger and impatience in his voice. "Mother, you know very well Donny's a friend of mine."

"Oh, you and your friends." Agatha waved a dismissal.

"He's been a big help in all this," Hedges defended.

"Stop!" Lee shouted. "I'm telling this." She looked at me, and her tone softened. "Kyle, the simple fact of the matter is that for four years, I've been in love with you." She sat down in the chair nearest me.

"Do you remember the first time we met?" Lee asked.

I nodded.

"I had read a column you wrote for that now defunct fanzine, *Make Mine Mystery*, and I had been really impressed. So I tracked you down and invited you to lunch at the Waldorf. Remember?"

I nodded again.

"It was the most wonderful meal of my life." Lee smiled. "And the longest. We sat in the restaurant for four hours, and you talked most of the time. You explained how you came up with the name Stokes Moran. Remember? That the first mystery story you ever read was Sherlock Holmes and *The Adventure of the Speckled Band*. And that the village or the house, I forget which, was called Stoke Moran. So you just added an 's' to Stoke and took the name to show your love for mysteries. Remember?"

I nodded for the third time.

"You also told me that day all about your childhood, the tragedies with your parents, your sense of abandonment, your loneliness. Your feelings were so intense, so intimate. We were total strangers, but you opened up to me. And I thought, here is a man I could fall in love with. Which is just what happened."

Lee stood up. "But it never went any further than that. I became your agent, we worked together, we had other lunches. But that was it. No romance." She glared at me, a hurt and accusing note in her voice.

"For four years you've completely ignored me. You lived in that safe little world of yours, in your tight little cocoon, isolated from everybody, complete in yourself. I couldn't break through. Well, I was getting sick of it." Lee began to pace, walking a circle around my chair. I craned my neck to follow her.

"Then, the Saturday after this Thanksgiving, I was watching *Romancing the Stone*—"

"Oh, I just love that movie," Agatha interjected, but Lee continued, ignoring the interruption. "And it suddenly dawned on me. You were exactly like the Kathleen Turner character in that movie. You were both living in your own worlds of make-believe. But she changed, and I realized you could change too."

Lee stopped her pacing, standing once more in front of my chair. "And what changed her was an adventure. So I decided you'd have an adventure too—but one where I got to play the Michael Douglas part." Lee reached out and cupped my chin.

"I know this sounds silly, darling, but I was desperate. So I spent the next few days working on the plot for our adventure. Just like I do for my books." I suppose Lee saw the sudden interest on my face.

"The only things that really interest you are mysteries. And I had a helluva one just perfect for the occasion—who was Seymour Severe? I knew that would get your attention."

Lee started pacing again. "But I had one little problem. After four years of nothing, I wasn't sure your lack of interest in me was merely your preoccupation with your own separate existence or if maybe it indicated a more complete rejection of the female persuasion. In other words, I thought you might be gay."

I started to speak, but Lee waved me silent.

"After our recent intimacy, I realize that was a totally wrong assumption. But you were so nonresponsive to what I felt were some pretty obvious indications of my attraction to you that— I suppose as a defense mechanism—I imagined you must be homosexual. But I couldn't be sure."

"Why didn't you just ask me?" I finally spoke.

"That sounds like such a simple question," Lee said.

"It is a simple question," I retorted.

"But it doesn't address my basic insecurity."

I laughed. "You? Insecure? Not bloody likely."

"Oh, but that's where you're wrong." I heard a wistfulness, a certain sadness, in Lee's voice. "Just like I didn't know the real you, you didn't know the real me." Lee closed her eyes for a moment.

"Professionally I may come on like gangbusters." I nodded assent. "But privately I live as much a secluded and lonely life as you do."

Could it be true? Not Lee, not the ferocious contract negotiator, not the eternal optimist, not the blood-and-guts novelist Seymour Severe.

"Oh yes," she said, as if reading my thoughts. "You are a reader. I am a writer. Both extremely solitary lives."

She walked over to Matthew Hedges.

"But I needed help to put my plan into action. So I made perhaps the biggest mistake of my life. I enlisted the aid of my brother."

Hedges frowned but voiced no objection.

"Matty is the most openly gay man I know. His experiences have provided me with a lot of insight into that alternate lifestyle." Lee paused, then added, "Not to mention material for my books." She smiled affectionately at her brother, and he smiled back.

"So," she continued, "I knew if anybody could determine your sexual preference, Matty could."

"Thanks a lot," I said sarcastically.

Matty nodded. "Think nothing of it."

"And he was the one who added murder to the plot,"she said.

Lee turned again to me. "At first, I rejected the idea. I thought it would just complicate things. But the more I thought about it, the more I liked it. Why not put you in the middle of a murder mystery? A reader of mysteries forced into living one? It was perfect. But it had to be a murder mystery without a real murder." Lee smiled. "There were certain limits beyond which even I wouldn't go."

I laughed, despite myself. And so did Matty, Manny, and Donny. Agatha appeared to be dozing.

"Matty said he'd take care of everything. The only thing he needed help with was the makeup so it'd look believable. So I enlisted Mark's help for that."

I said "Ah."

"Yes, you saw the same thing at Mark's studio. Now, with Matty ready to go here in New Orleans, all I had to do was get you interested, so I invented the story about *Playboy* wanting an exposé on Seymour Severe."

This shocked me. "You mean that wasn't true either?"

Lee shook her head.

"Then who's been footing all the bills?"

"I have," Lee laughed. "I got a million-dollar advance for the new Severe. And this little adventure's not going to cost but about ten thousand. So if it's accomplished what I hope it's accomplished, I consider it money well spent."

Lee leaned against the railing.

"So I sent you on your merry way, into the unreliable hands of my brother. I left all the details here in New Orleans to Matty. I didn't exactly know what he was going to do, but I knew he'd pull it off. And when he called to tell me I had a repressed heterosexual on my hands"—I could imagine how Matty had phrased that—"and were on your way back home, it was up to me to take it from there.

"And suddenly, I was having second thoughts.

"For the first time, it hit me—the enormity of what I'd done. It had all seemed so easy, so safe in the planning. But when I saw you, when you told me what had happened, I realized you'd been through an emotional wringer, that Matty had gone too far. And what if you hated me for it? I knew sooner or later you'd find out the truth. Revealing the plot had been part of the plan all along. And that terrified me.

"I almost backed out. But the clues had already been planted. Just like a good mystery writer, I wanted to play fair. And I knew if I gave you enough time to think about it, you'd eventually figure it out. So I had to keep things moving. Like it or not."

Lee sat in the chair she'd vacated earlier.

"But you surprised me. You started behaving differently than I had expected. For one thing, you turned into a thief."

She smiled. "Sometimes when I'm writing my Giles Manning adventures, a character will take on a life of his own and dictate action I hadn't expected. And you did the same thing. You weren't bound by the plot I had created for you. You just stubbornly refused to cooperate with how I had scripted it."

Her facial expression changed from smile to frown. "And there was one other thing I had not fully appreciated. In planning an adventure for you, I had also planned one for myself. And I didn't want to leave my safe little cocoon either. You see, I had lived with the fantasy so long that I was afraid of the reality. What if my plan didn't work? What if you just weren't attracted to me? What if I lost you completely?

"The possibilities were really scary. But the alternatives were even worse. I couldn't leave you hanging like that, believing you had killed someone. And I knew I couldn't continue with my one-sided love affair. Not with what I'd done to you always there between us, even if you never found out. So, whether you hated me for it or not, I had to go on." Lee's energy drained from her features. "The only difference was that I knew what we were getting into, and you didn't."

Lee yawned. "But I had started this, and I had to finish it. That's just about it. I'm tired. I think you can fill in the rest." She looked at me expectantly. When I didn't immediately respond, she asked, "Don't you have anything to say?"

"Yes." I turned to Matthew Hedges. "Gimme a cigarette."

C H A P T E R 2 2

*"Not since Ellery Queen took pen in hand to
relate his own cases has an author so enter-
tained the reader with his own exploits."*
            —Stokes Moran,
   on Kinky Friedman's Greenwich Killing Time

Like all good mystery novels, the clues had been there all
along, and a careful reading would have revealed the solution.
I had just been too dumb to see it. The questions that had
plagued me for the past few days now had answers—at least
some of them did.

How had Matthew Hedges known I would be coming to
New Orleans in the first place? Lee had told him, that's how.

How had he known I was looking for Seymour Severe?
Again, Lee.

That I would be getting twenty-five thousand dollars for the
story? That I was working on my own mystery novel? All Lee.

"Were the police in on it too?" That was the first question I
asked aloud after taking a long drag from the cigarette Matty
had provided and lit, after which he had considerately handed me an ashtray.

"No. That was the one gamble we took." Lee answered
matter-of-factly. Her voice sounded dead, without animation,
without emotion. "But as overworked as our police forces are,

I felt that once we had our son back"—was she still acting out the fiction?—"that would be the end of their involvement."

"Why go through the charade of changing my appearance?" I asked the questions with no logical progression, merely as they occurred to me.

"I wanted to see how determined you were to follow this thing through. I knew if you put up with all Mark's machinations, you were really hooked. Plus Mark had the means to do it, it added a little spice to my script, and it gave us more time together."

"More time together?"

"Yeah." Lee stood up and leaned against the runway. "The way I figured it, the more time we spent together, the greater our chances at intimacy, at finally getting beyond that invisible barrier that had held our relationship in check for four years."

I doubted that two weeks ago Lee could have voiced those thoughts aloud, either to herself or to me, let alone in front of other people. And I know I couldn't have listened. But circumstances had changed. Boy, had they changed.

Right now, the dialogue was strictly Lee's and mine. The other players had dropped out. Matthew Hedges and Manny Gillis sat quietly in their chairs, Agatha continued to doze, and Donny remained separate from the rest of the group, standing on the runway, leaning against the far wall. Yes, the scene by necessity belonged just to Lee and me.

"Kyle, are you angry? Can you forgive me?" Lee ventured.

Good questions. Did I even know how I felt? I remembered feeling angry earlier. Hurt? I suppose there was a certain amount of hurt, mostly to my pride, however. Surprised? Yes, that too. Astonished really. So in the moment before I answered Lee's questions, I defined for myself my tangled emotions and feelings. Finally, I spoke.

"No, Lee, I'm not angry." For the first time since waking in this room, I rose from my chair. I walked over to where Lee was standing. "And there's nothing to forgive, unless you can forgive my blind stupidity for the past four years." She rushed into my outstretched arms, and we kissed.

A sudden light seemed to fill the room, and it didn't come from the new day dawning outside since the room had no windows. Immediate activity greeted our reunion.

Matthew Hedges slapped me on the back. "No hard feelings?" He extended his right hand.

"Not at all." I accepted his gesture of friendship and clasped Lee to my side. "If you want to know the truth, and this may sound crazy, but I'm flattered. Flattered that anyone," and I hugged Lee, "would go to so much trouble just for me."

Manny Gillis and I shook hands as well. "There aren't many people who get to have a complete mystery story created just for them," he agreed.

Agatha, now fully awake, kissed me on the cheek, and Donny finally broke his aloofness and joined the group.

"This feels like a celebration." Lee laughed. Tears streaked her mascara.

"It is, darling." Agatha embraced her daughter. "Even if we're all dead with sleep, it's a party."

"Could I get a few things cleared up in my mind?" I asked.

"Sure," Lee said.

"First, what are you all doing here at this hour of the morning? Do you all live in this house together?"

Matthew Hedges answered. "No. Mother is the only one who actually lives here all the time. Manny lives over the bookstore, and Donny stays with me in my apartment on Chartres."

"Then what were you doing here at four in the morning?"

"Unlike you, we weren't breaking and entering." He laughed. "As a matter of fact, the three of us"—he indicated himself, Manny, and Donny—"were just bringing over a little something from Manny's shop."

"At that hour of the morning?" I interrupted.

"That's the shank of the evening for me." Then Matty continued, "And weren't we surprised when we discovered a burglar in the library!"

I let that pass and decided instead to voice my next question.

"And this is Fido's?"

Matty nodded. "But not really," he added. "Fido's was just part of the plan. And it was quicker than seduction." He winked at me again. I didn't appreciate the familiarity, not with all I now knew about him.

"But I saw people here," I asserted.

"Let's just say I'm a member of a gentlemen's club, and leave it at that."

Some club, I thought, and Matthew Hedges was certainly no gentleman. But I decided not to pursue the point.

"So who was Minerva?" I asked. "Was she part of all this?"

"*You tell Matty to stay away from Donny,*" Matty mimicked in falsetto. "*He's my son.*"

"You! I'll be damned."

After the laughter subsided, I asked my next question.

"And who or what is Duchess Court?"

Again Hedges answered. "Ever since childhood, my nick-
name for Lee has been Dutch." Of course, Holland—how
could I have missed it? Hedges grinned. "I sent that little clue
by way of Donny. Orally, it sounds like duchess court. But
when you write it out, it reads Dutch's court. 'Now the ball's
in Dutch's court.' But I wasn't sure I should use it. I thought it
might be overplaying the hand a bit."

"Not with this feeble brain," I admitted.

"So it stumped you?" He seemed pleased.

"Oh yes."

I then looked directly at Donny. "How do you fit in?" I
asked him. "Are you a member of the family?"

"Not officially," said Matthew Hedges, and he walked over
to Donny and placed his arm around the boy's shoulders.
"Donny and I are just friends." The proprietorial manner in
which the two men looked at each other defined for me their
true relationship.

"Very close friends," Donny added and rested his hand on
Matty's shoulder.

I reminded myself that Donny, even though he looked like a
child, was an adult, legally at least, and that he had chosen his
lifestyle. I wondered how much of the personal history he had
shared with me in the hotel room had been the truth. I
guessed, quite a lot. But the familiarity between Matty and
Donny continued to bother me. I finally decided it was the age
difference, more than anything else.

"Is now a good time for the gift?" Manny asked Lee. She
nodded. The big man climbed the steps to the runway, disappeared for a minute behind the screen, and returned carting a

211

cardboard box. He bent down from the stage and handed it to me.

"From Lee," he said.

The box was not heavy, and I could cradle it in one arm while lifting up the folded flaps with my other hand. The first thing I saw was the dust jacket of *Farewell, My Lovely*.

"It's all the books that were in the bottom drawer of Manny's filing cabinet," Lee explained. "And one other."

I was stunned. Here was a treasure beyond imagination.

"Why?" was all I could say.

"I've been collecting them for you for the past four years. I knew you'd never buy them for yourself, and I also knew you'd never accept them as gifts. Your male pride or New England practicality would never have allowed that."

"Well, what makes you think I will take them now?"

"Just think of them as a wedding gift." There was still a touch of uncertainty, of vulnerability in Lee's voice.

"A wedding gift?"

Lee laughed. "Yes, remember I'm no longer shy."

"I can see that." I kissed her softly on the lips, shifting the box awkwardly to the side. "Thank you," I whispered.

"Why don't we all go downstairs to the kitchen and fix some breakfast," Agatha suggested. "If we have to be up at this ungodly hour, let's at least eat."

Everybody laughed, and the group headed to the stairs. I held Lee back.

"You said 'one other.' What did you mean?"

Lee pushed the box toward the floor, reached into it, scrounged around for a minute, then pulled *The Pale Horse* into view. I smiled, and leaned over to kiss her again.

"How did you just happen to have these books here?"

"I knew the eventual resolution of our little play would take place here," Lee said. "So I told Manny that as soon as you'd gone through the drawer to box the books up and bring them here. I told Sheila—that's Manny's assistant—to add *The Pale Horse* while you were in the back room stealing the manuscript."

"And speaking of that manuscript," I said, "just what is the title of the new Seymour Severe?"

"Don't you know that's the most closely guarded secret in publishing history," Lee joked.

"Won't you even tell me?" Then, I added, "Your future husband?"

"Husband?"

I nodded.

"In that case," Lee smiled, "I guess it's okay." She slipped her hand in mine. "I'm calling it *Otherwise Known as Murder.*"

"Good title," I said. I released Lee's hand and hefted the box of books up onto my right shoulder.

"I'm glad you like it," Lee answered, snuggling easily under my left arm. "Now let's get home to Bootsie."